BROKEN

ELIZABETH KELLY

EK PUBLISHING INC.

Edited by:
L. Nunn Editing

Cover art by
The Final Wrap

BROKEN

Ugly...monster...freak.

Ford Taylor has endured the whispers and the horrified stares his entire life. Rejected by both his family and strangers for how he looks, he's grown accustomed to his lonely life. His life is changed forever when Stella, the redheaded beauty he harbours a secret crush on, befriends him.

Photographer Stella Johnson is fascinated by the quiet man with the unconventional looks. Her sweet nature and ability to see Ford for who he really is slowly break down the walls he's built around his heart. Their friendship soon blossoms into love.

But when Ford's insecurities and a dark secret from his past threaten their relationship, Stella must convince him that their love for each other is the only thing that matters.

* * *

For a FREE Elizabeth Kelly short story, as well as excerpts of upcoming books and contests and giveaways, sign up for Elizabeth's newsletter here

PROLOGUE

H is face was one that only a mother could love. An odd mixture of harsh corners and ridges and awkward, oversized features. In truth, his mother didn't love him. She was perplexed and a little horrified by the child she had birthed. To have this red-faced, oddly silent creature come sliding out of her after the perfection that was her firstborn made her more than a little uneasy.

Later, long after her husband had returned to their home and the nurses had left her room, she held her baby in her arms and studied each feature silently. He was ugly. She couldn't - hadn't wanted to - deny it. The looks on the nurses' faces, the grimace from her husband when he had first surveyed his new son, had filled her with an odd kind of shame as if she and she alone were to blame for the monstrosity she had given birth to.

As he grew into a man and his body filled out to become an impressive and unforgiving block of sinewy muscle and harsh strength, her unease turned to fear. It didn't matter that he was gentle and quiet or that her dislike and fear obviously crushed him. He had the face and body of a man who would use his fists instead of his words to solve his problems, and she cringed away from his fumbled attempts to win her love.

Eventually, he gave up. He retreated into his own world and bore his family's repulsion toward him with a stoic solemnity. His weekly visits turned to monthly, and neither she nor his father and siblings could hide their relief.

He found solace in books, in art, and with the few friends he made. Friends who didn't care that nature had played so cruelly with his looks or that he was so quiet one would almost believe he was mute. His life was good, if not a bit lonely, and he was content.

Until he met her.

CHAPTER 1

Stella Johnson pressed the lobby button and rubbed at her back as the doors slid shut and the elevator carried her smoothly and efficiently down thirty-seven floors. The doors opened with a soft ding, and she walked briskly toward the atrium to the left of the front doors, holding her lunch bag in her hand.

Her stomach growled softly, and she patted her round tummy before smoothing her dress. It was one of her favourites. A chocolate brown maxi dress that clung to her full breasts but flared out around her stomach and wide hips. It fell to the middle of her calves as most of her dresses did. She liked to hide the depressing way her thighs touched, and she preferred to dress conservatively anyway.

Her shoes click-clacked on the tile floor of the lobby. Bright red and with a heel too high for the office, she loved them with the same passion she imagined a mother might feel for her child. Ridiculous, of course, but her love for shoes came by her naturally. Her mother had close to two hundred pairs of shoes, and Stella was certain not a single one of them had a heel less than two inches high.

3

"Stelll-lllaaa!"

She grinned at the short, blond man sitting behind the security desk. "Hello, Jimmy. How are you?"

"Can't complain. Well, I could, but no one would listen." He stood and stretched. "You're running late today."

"Amy had an appointment," she said.

"Enjoy your lunch."

"I will." She hid her small grin as his face suddenly lit up, and he hurried around the desk. She didn't need to look behind her to know that Jasmine, the owner of the small flower shop in the lobby, was walking behind her. The woman was a gorgeous piece of art. Slim and tanned with bright pink hair that should have looked ridiculous on someone her age but didn't.

A month ago, Stella had coaxed Jasmine into sitting for her. She'd snapped photo after photo of the pink-haired beauty and was delighted with the results. Jasmine was a natural with the camera, and Stella hoped she could convince her to sit for her again.

The entire security team in the building constantly vied for Jasmine's attention. As Jimmy said hello to Jasmine in a tone entirely different from the one he used with her, Stella smoothed back her own hair.

She knew it was her best feature. Dark red, it was a thick, curly mass that flowed down her back to her waist. Men and women alike complimented her on it daily. Although truthfully, she didn't always understand the appeal. She longed for smooth, straight, dark hair. She'd almost cut it short last year, but her boyfriend at the time was horrified by the idea.

"Your hair is beautiful, Stella," he'd said earnestly as they lay in bed. "If you cut it off, the only thing people will notice about you is the extra weight you carry around. Do you want people to comment on the size of your ass instead of your hair?"

4

He hadn't understood her indignation. He honestly thought he was complimenting her. The relationship limped along for a few more weeks until she finally ended it. Although she was self-confident and mostly happy with her looks, her weight had always been a sore spot.

She'd made an appointment at the hair salon to cut her hair but chickened out. She told herself it was because her hair had never been shorter than mid-back, and it would be too strange to see it otherwise. But her ex-boyfriend's words were always in the back of her mind.

She headed into the atrium, her gait slowing when she saw how full it was. She regularly took a late lunch, covering Amy's lunch break at reception before taking her own. She didn't mind. She liked the quietness of the atrium with the lunch crowd long gone.

Although it was never completely empty, there were always a few people milling about and Ford, one of the security guards, took his lunch at the same time. She suspected he also enjoyed the solitude, so she never spoke to him. Not that he even acknowledged her existence. He ate his lunch and then sat with a pencil and sketchpad in his hand. She was often tempted to sneak up behind him for a quick glance, but she didn't have the nerve despite her curiosity. He might wield a pencil instead of a camera, but he was an artist like her, and she would have liked to talk to him about his work.

Today, all the small tables were full, and the loud chatter of people echoed in the atrium. She thought briefly of taking her lunch outside to the small park across the street, but the storm that was threatening when she arrived at work now lashed rain against the windows of the atrium.

Her gaze landed on Ford. He sat at his usual table, hunched over his sketchpad, ignoring the curious glances of the people sitting at the closest table. She had a feeling that he learned at an early age to ignore the looks and the whispers.

There was an empty chair at his table. Stella wasn't surprised. She doubted anyone would have the courage to approach him and ask to sit at his table. If the sheer size of his body and the obvious hard line of his muscles didn't deter them, his unconventional looks definitely did.

Gathering her courage, she weaved between the small tables scattered across the atrium until she stood before him. Engrossed in his sketch, he didn't look up. She cleared her throat and tugged nervously at her hair. "Hello, Ford."

She strained to see what he was drawing. It looked like a portrait, a woman with large eyes and high cheekbones and —

He put his arm over the drawing, blocking it neatly with his large forearm. He gave her a quick, fleeting glance. "Hello, Stella."

"Would you mind if I shared your table? The atrium is busy today."

He made a small backward twitch as if he were simply going to stand up and walk away before nodding. "Go ahead."

She sat down as he slid his sketchpad into the large fabric bag that served as his lunch bag. He pulled out an apple, a banana, an orange, a block of cheese as thick as her wrist, a plastic container filled to the brim with roast beef, two hard boiled eggs, and a large muffin.

She opened her lunch bag and brought out her lunch. A small garden salad with an even tinier container of raw almonds that she sprinkled over the salad. Ford opened his container, and the smell of roast beef drifted across the table to her. Her stomach growled, and he gave her another one of those quick glances as she blushed.

"Sorry, apparently I'm hungry today."

She nibbled at her salad, forcing herself to chew slowly as Ford ate his lunch. They sat silently as she finished her salad and put away her container. Normally, she would pull out her book and spend the rest of her lunch hour reading, but it seemed rude when she was sharing a table, even if Ford hadn't said a word to her.

She looked up as two women she'd never seen before stopped a few feet from their table. They stared at Ford with curiosity and undisguised pity, and she glared frostily at them until they moved on.

If Ford noticed their stares it didn't seem to affect him. Stella stared at her neatly painted fingernails. She'd worked in the building for nearly six months, and this was the first time she'd really gotten a good look at his face. Well, as good as she could with him staring grimly at the table.

She wondered if he would be surprised to know how much she wanted to photograph him. She was fascinated by the shapes and contours of his face. While others called him ugly, she thought his face was unique – almost beautiful in its ugliness.

Her stomach growled again, and Ford finally raised his gaze to her. She studied his face - the harsh angles, the bulbous nose, the heavy brow, and the black stubble that grew on his cheeks.

"You don't eat enough."

"I'm sorry?" She blinked at him.

"Every day, you eat a salad that wouldn't be enough to fill up a rabbit. You need more protein."

"I put raw almonds in it," she said.

He snorted. "A few almonds aren't a sufficient amount of protein. Protein fuels the body and the muscles."

She grinned at him. "I haven't got any muscles."

"Everyone has muscles."

"All right, fine. My muscles aren't as well-defined as

yours, and probably don't need half a roast beef to make them happy. How often do you work out, anyway?" She eyed how his shirt hugged his broad chest and pulled at his shoulders and arms.

"Every day," he grunted.

"Shocking." She glanced around the atrium. "It's busy in here today."

"The law office on the seventeenth floor is having some kind of conference."

"Oh." She cast about for something else to say. She was a talker, always had been, and Ford's silence unnerved her a bit. "You like to draw, huh?"

He gave her a cautious look before nodding and biting into his apple.

"I'm a photographer. Well, amateur, but I love it. I mostly take portraits. I convinced Jasmine to sit for me a few weeks ago."

He glanced over to where Jimmy and Jasmine were still conversing in the lobby.

"Someone's got a crush." Stella grinned.

He grunted and stuffed his empty lunch containers and trash into the fabric bag.

"So, have you been drawing since you were a kid?"

He pushed back his chair and stood. "Lunch break's over. Bye."

"Bye, Ford."

He didn't return her smile. She watched him walk away as people naturally moved out of the way of his large body. She took her book out of her lunch bag and wondered what it must be like to be that intimidating. To never have to throw a thought toward personal safety. She was tall and weighed more than she would have liked, but she was also as weak as a kitten. She was being honest when she told Ford she didn't have muscles. He opened the door behind the security desk and disappeared into the office. With a soft sigh, she opened her book and blocked out the sounds of the chatting and laughter around her.

* * *

FORD CRAMMED HIS MASSIVE BODY BEHIND THE TINY DESK IN the office and stared at his hands. He wasn't surprised to see them shaking. She had talked to him. He had an actual conversation with her. Well, if you called telling her she didn't eat enough, a conversation.

He didn't think she would show up at the atrium today. She was late, and he'd already resigned himself to the fact that his brief glimpse of her this morning would be it for the day unless he happened to see her as she was leaving.

A small thrill went through him when she'd finally shown up with her lunch bag in hand and wearing his favourite dress. When she had actually approached him, tugging on a strand of that amazing, flame-coloured hair, and asked to join him, he'd nearly run like a startled deer.

Staring at her from a distance was a completely different experience from having her sitting across the table. Ford hoped she didn't get a good look at his sketch. He was certain that women didn't like the idea of a man drawing secret pictures of them.

He was ridiculously pleased that she shared information with him. He knew she liked to take photos. He'd heard Jasmine telling Jimmy about it at the security desk and caught a glimpse of the pictures Jasmine showed Jimmy. Stella was good, and Ford admired her ability.

He took a deep breath. Christ, she smelled good, like a combination of vanilla and some type of flower. He was struck by how she'd looked at him as if she noticed the ugli-ness of his features but wasn't horrified by it like so many other people were. He rubbed his forehead. Thinking that she didn't mind his looks was a bad idea. Women were disgusted by him, even someone as sweet as Stella.

Ford's stomach tightened painfully, and he stood up and returned to the front desk. Stella sat with him today because she had no choice, and that was it. His pointless crush on her needed to end.

CHAPTER 2

"Hello, Ford."

This time, she didn't ask to join him. She just plopped down in the chair across from him as if it belonged to her, as the scent of vanilla floated across the table.

"Hey, Stella."

"How long is the conference supposed to go on for, do you know?" She rummaged in her lunch bag and pulled out her usual salad and container of almonds. He looked away hurriedly when she bent and deposited her bag on the floor beside her. Her shirt had caught between her arm and her body and pulled her modest neckline down. He had seen a glimpse of soft white skin and blue lace.

Did her panties match?

His mouth went dry at the thought of Stella standing in front of him in nothing but her bra and panties. He stared mutely at the tub of roast beef on the table.

"Ford?"

He grunted something hoarse and unintelligible at her, and she frowned. "Are you all right?"

"Yeah."

"Are you sure? You have a weird look on your face."

"I'm fine." He cleared his throat and took a long drink of water.

She eyed him carefully, and he thought he saw actual concern on her face before she cleared her own throat. "So, do you know?"

Like a horny teenage boy, he was still stuck on the glimpse of her breast and of the blue lace that covered it. She was sensible and conservative in the way she dressed, preferring long skirts and modest shirts and jackets that covered her breasts. Her shoes, though - they were a completely different story. Jimmy referred to them as stripper shoes, and Ford supposed they were.

She wore ridiculously high heels completely impractical for walking in. In the six months she'd worked in the building, he had never seen her in shoes that didn't have at least two-inch heels. They brought her impressive height to nearly six feet, and she towered over half the security team. Not him, though. At just shy of 6' 6", he hadn't met anyone who came close to his height.

Today, she wore shoes with a skinny heel that made him wince just to think about walking in them. Her shoes matched her bra in colour. Did her panties match, too?

Maybe. Ask her out on a date. Maybe you'll find out for yourself if her panties match her bra.

He jerked when Stella's soft hand touched the top of his. "Ford?"

He closed his eyes, took a deep breath, and forced his mind out of the gutter. "Do I know what?"

"How long the conference lasts?" She stared at him tentatively, like she thought he might just stand up and bolt. While he couldn't force himself to smile at her, he nodded in what he hoped was a friendly manner.

"Uh, yeah. It goes all week."

"Oh." She glanced around the crowded atrium before taking a bite of her salad. She didn't even put dressing on it, for God's sake. He took a huge bite of his roast beef as she sipped at her water and then smiled at him.

"Well, I guess you're stuck with me all week then. Lucky you." She wiggled her eyebrows at him before popping an almond in her mouth and smiling. He stared at her lips and felt another rush of heat hit his groin.

Shit, he really needed to get control of himself. He grimaced, and the smile fell from her face.

"I'm sorry. I can sit somewhere else. It was rude of me to assume that -"

"No, it's fine." The words popped out of his mouth before he could stop them. He didn't want her sitting with him. It was way too torturous. But he couldn't stand the thought of hurting her feelings either.

Sweat beading up on his brow, he tried to smile at her, but it must have come out as a grimace because she gave him another embarrassed look.

"Really, I don't mind sitting somewhere else. I know you like your privacy, and I understand."

He shook his head, panic threading through him when she started to stand. "No! It's fine, Stella!"

His voice echoed through the atrium. He turned bright red as the babble of conversations stopped, and nearly everyone in the atrium turned to look at them. He bent his head and stared at the table as Stella cleared her throat and stared at the others. "What? You've never heard someone doing a *Streetcar Named Desire* impression before? Carry on. Nothing to see here, folks."

The murmur of conversations started up. Ford forced himself to stay still as Stella patted the top of his hand. "Sorry."

"It's fine," he mumbled.

She sat quietly and ate her salad as he picked at the roast beef in front of him. His stomach churned, knowing he'd made a fool of himself. She wouldn't sit with him again, and he couldn't blame her.

He wished desperately that he knew how to speak to a woman. In movies and television, the ugly guy was always charming with a self-deprecating sense of humour that eventually made women find him attractive.

Unfortunately, he was shy. Even if he'd been normal looking, he would have been quiet and nervous. His ugliness had turned him into an introvert bordering on complete social disaster.

"So, do you cook an entire roast beef daily, or is that leftovers?" Stella sounded unsure and nervous, and he sighed inwardly. He was really fucking this up.

"Leftovers."

"Right. You eat a lot of meat, huh? You like meat?"

Before he could answer, she turned bright red and slapped herself on the forehead. "Oh my God, Stella! Could you be any more awkward? Ford, I swear I'm not normally this stupid."

"I don't think you're stupid," he said.

"What kind of idiot asks a guy about his meat?" She stared at him, and he suspected a grin was creeping over his face.

She quickly ate the rest of her salad. When the container was empty, she eyed his roast beef before taking another sip of water.

"Here." He placed a thick slab of beef on the lid of her container.

"Ford, no, you don't have to -"

"You don't eat enough," he said. "How do you even make it through the afternoon without passing out?"

"Caffeine and cheese," she said.

He arched his eyebrow at her, and she shrugged. "I like coffee, and I love cheese. It's got protein, right?"

"Yeah," he said grudgingly.

"Still," she eyed the slab of beef on her container, "this does look delicious. Do you know how long it's been since I've had meat?"

She suddenly blushed furiously. "Oh, Jesus. I didn't mean – I meant red meat, not like man meat."

This time, he knew he was grinning. Stella was apparently standing right next to him in the gutter.

She groaned and slapped herself again on the forehead. "Man meat! I cannot believe I just said man meat."

She took a deep breath and blew it out. "Stop saying man meat, Stella."

Her smile embarrassed, she said, "I haven't eaten red meat in a really long time."

"Why not?"

She shrugged. "I heard it wasn't that good for you."

"It's fine in moderation."

"I guess," she agreed. "But I live by myself, and if I cooked an entire roast beef, I'd probably eat it in less than two days. But unlike with you, it'll increase my ass size, not my muscle size."

She grinned at him, and he rolled his eyes. "You don't eat enough."

"You keep mentioning that," she said. "But I haven't passed out yet from lack of food, so I think I'm okay."

"Just eat the roast beef, Stella." He stared at her in exasperation, and she laughed.

"Yes, sir."

Using her fingers, she tore off a piece and popped it into her mouth. "Oh my God," she mumbled, "that's really good."

They ate in silence, and his groin stirred when she licked

her fingers clean. "This is delicious. Did you cook that yourself?"

He nodded and bit into his apple as she sat back in her chair. "You're a great cook."

"Thanks."

They sat in silence for a few minutes, and he could feel himself starting to sweat. He was terrible at small talk. The longer they sat there, the more desperate he began to feel. Stella would leave if he didn't say something soon.

"So, uh, you're a photographer?" he said.

Her eyes lit up, and she leaned forward, resting her chin on her hands. "I am. Just an amateur one, but I love it. I'm trying to make a career of it. I'm always looking for new people to photograph. My family and friends are sick to death of me taking their pictures. My dad won't even come to my place now because he knows I'll trap him in my studio for a portrait session."

"You have a studio?"

"Well, I call it my studio. It's actually just my spare room that I set up with my camera equipment."

"How long have you been taking pictures?"

"I got my first camera when I was twelve, and I've been hooked on it ever since. I love how a good portrait can capture a person's spirit. You know? I love using natural light for photography. Sometimes, when I can't find more victims to photograph among my friends and family, I do street photography. I'm not that great at it, though. You need to have nerves of steel to take pictures of random strangers."

He watched her mouth as she talked animatedly. Something about the curve of Stella's mouth and how her eyes sparkled when she talked drove him almost crazy with need. She talked a lot, but he didn't mind. He spent most of his social engagements trying to think of something to say, and it was a bit of a relief to sit back and listen. He could listen to her voice and stare at her mouth all day.

He finished eating his lunch, nodding and even smiling occasionally as she spoke about photography and her family. She seemed to really enjoy spending time with them. He wondered what it was like to have a mother and father who looked forward to seeing you.

He didn't realize how quickly time had passed until Stella reached into her bag and pulled out her cell phone. She checked the time and jumped up.

"Crap! I'm going to be late. I've gotta run, Ford. Have a great day, and I'll see you tomorrow, okay?" She waved at him as she click-clacked on those ridiculous heels across the foyer to the elevator.

He took a deep breath and returned to the security desk. His heart was pounding, and he was having a hard time keeping a grin from his face. Jimmy punched him lightly in the arm.

"Ford, you okay, man?"

"Yeah, why?"

Jimmy shrugged. "You look weird."

"No, I don't." He scowled at Jimmy, and the younger man laughed.

"There we go. That's the Ford I'm used to seeing. God, buddy, you almost looked happy for a minute there. It was freaking me out."

* * *

"I thought you said a salad wasn't enough food." Stella eyed his large container of greens as she sat across from him.

His heart skipped a beat. The conference had ended on Friday, and the atrium was back to its normal, almost empty

17

ELIZABETH KELLY

self. He'd sat at his usual table, resigned that his lunches with Stella were over.

It doesn't mean anything. She's just being friendly.

"No, I said *your* salad wasn't enough," he said.

"We have the exact same salad," she said. "You have almonds in yours. Maybe I should be lecturing you about passing out this afternoon."

He reached across and dumped a portion of his salad into her container. "It also has cranberries, walnuts, and a lot more vegetables. A properly made salad gives you lots of energy and," he stared sternly at her, "keeps you from passing out."

She grinned cheekily before taking a bite. "Ooh, this dressing is delicious. What is it?"

"A raspberry vinaigrette."

"I need to buy some. Where did you get it?"

"I made it."

"Really? Damn, you should consider a career as a chef. I'd totally hire you to be my personal chef," she said.

He had a sudden image of standing in Stella's kitchen. In his mind, the kitchen was small and intimate. There would be no way to stop from brushing up against each other as he cooked and listened to her chat about her day.

"What are you so happy about all of a sudden?" Stella paused with a forkful of salad held at her mouth.

He blinked and forced the smile from his face. "Nothing."

"You like the idea of being a chef," she announced. "Maybe you should do it."

"I like being a security guard," he said.

"Do you?" She cocked her head at him. "Or are you like me, where it's something to pay the bills while you figure out how to do what you love for a living?"

He shrugged. "I don't know what you're talking about."

"Bullshit," she said cheerfully. "You're always drawing in

18

that sketch pad. I bet you're an amazing artist. Can I see a few of your sketches?"

His cheeks went red. Considering that lately, every single one of his drawings was of Stella, there was no way in hell he was showing her his work.

"I'm not good," he said.

"Oh, c'mon," she wheedled. "I'll show you some of my photos if you show me some of your drawings."

He shook his head. "They're nothing special, trust me."

Her adorable pout made his cock stir in his pants. She sat back and twirled a lock of that amazing hair around one finger. "Have you always worked in security?"

"No."

She waited patiently, and after a moment, he said, "I'm ex-military."

"Not surprised," she said. "What did you do?"

"I was in the Marines."

Her mouth dropped open, and he stared at her bottom lip before forcing his gaze back to his salad.

"Wow. They're like the best of the best, right?" Stella said.

He shrugged, and she leaned forward. "Ford, be honest with me. Can you kill a man with your bare hands?"

A grin crossed his face. "Why? Is there someone bothering you?"

"Well, Rick in accounting has been a bit of an ass lately," she said. "But killing him seems a little extreme, I guess. Maybe I'll just tell him I have a friend who's a Marine. That will straighten him out."

A stupid rush of pleasure went through him – she had referred to him as her friend.

She cocked her head at him. "Why did you leave? You're pretty young to retire from the military."

"I was tired of it," he lied.

She stared silently at him, and he cleared his throat. "A mission went bad, and a lot of my team died."

"You blamed yourself," she said.

"No," he said. It was the truth. He didn't blame himself. He had survivor's guilt. Hell, all four of them who made it out alive did. But they supported each other, and they all went through intense therapy afterward. It made a difference.

"Good," she said.

"I just – I was tired of the violence and the death. It was time to quit."

"Fair enough," she said. "I can't even begin to imagine the dangerous situations you've been in."

There was an awkward silence, and, as usual, she hurried to cover it. "I've never done anything dangerous in my life. I have a low tolerance for risk that might involve injury or death."

"Are you sure?" he said. "Those shoes look pretty high risk to me."

She laughed and held out her foot, admiring the strappy silver sandal with the high, tapered heel. "I've never so much as twisted an ankle, and you have to admit they look great."

He studied her feet, sweat breaking out on his brow as he imagined Stella in his bed wearing nothing but those heels. How it would feel to have them digging into his back as he knelt between her thighs and buried himself balls-deep inside of her.

"Ford? Are you all right? You have a weird look on your face."

"I'm fine," he rasped. He wanted desperately to leave, but that single image of Stella in his bed wearing only her high-heeled shoes had given him one hell of an erection. There was no way he could leave without her noticing. Jesus, he was acting like a sex-starved teenager.

"Okay," she said uncertainly. "Hey, are you going to the baseball game and barbeque this weekend?"

He stared at her in surprise. "Are you going?"

"Jimmy invited Jasmine and me to the security team's annual autumn baseball and barbeque event. I'm pretty certain Jimmy only invited me because I was standing with Jasmine when he asked her to go, and he didn't want to be rude."

She pulled self-consciously at her shirt. "Anyway, I said I would go because Jasmine wants me to, but I also don't want to be a third wheel. If you were going, the four of us could hang out together, and it wouldn't be so awkward."

"I'm going," he said.

He never went to the annual barbeque. As close as he was to the rest of the security team, he tended to avoid social gatherings. Especially ones where strangers would have the chance to gawk at him. But knowing Stella would be there and that he wouldn't have to go two days without seeing her was too difficult to resist.

"Awesome," she said happily as she tucked her empty food container into her lunch bag. "They want me to play in the baseball game too. How's that for crazy? I don't have an athletic bone in my body."

"Maybe don't wear your usual heels," he suggested.

She poked him playfully in the shoulder as she stood. "Thanks for the tip. Bye, Ford. I'll see you tomorrow, okay?"

"Yes. Bye, Stella."

CHAPTER 3

"Ford! Wait up!"

Balancing a casserole dish, a baseball glove, and a bat, Ford glanced behind him. Stella was hurrying across the parking lot, and he waited patiently for her. She wore yoga pants and a bulky sweatshirt, and her long hair was pulled into a ponytail.

"Hey, ready for the big game?" she asked when she caught up to him.

He nodded, and she glanced at the casserole dish. "What did you bring?"

"Macaroni and cheese."

"Yummy." She grinned at him before holding up the bag of buns in her left hand. "I brought buns. I made them fresh this morning."

"Sure, you did."

"Well, I'm sure the grocery store made them fresh this morning." Her giggle made him want to smile like a fool.

They walked toward the ball diamond. She adjusted the camera strap around her neck before showing him the glove she was carrying. "I borrowed my brother's glove. He almost fell over when I told him I was playing baseball."

"I'm sure you'll play just fine."

"Probably not," she said. "Did I mention my non-athletic body?"

"You did." He was helpless to stop his once-over of her body. Fuck, did her yoga pants have to be so tight?

"Do you like my shoes?" She seemed oblivious to his slow perusal.

"They're very shiny."

She whacked him playfully on the arm before studying her running shoes. They were bright pink with small, shiny beads covering their tops. "At least they're not heels."

"True," he said.

"So, who are we playing against?"

"The security team from the Myers building down the street."

"Cool."

They walked in comfortable silence to the diamond. The security team and their families were milling about, and he ignored the looks as they passed them. He placed the casserole dish on the already overloaded picnic table as Stella threw the bag of buns next to them.

He glanced at her. Her cheerful smile faded, and she glared at the woman standing at the end of the picnic table. The woman stared at him with curiosity and mild repulsion, and dull embarrassment went through him. He was used to the stares but knowing that Stella was seeing them made him want to turn tail and run. When it was just the two of them sitting together at lunch, it was almost easy to forget he was ugly. She *made* it easy with her odd obliviousness to his ugliness. But here, surrounded by people who made no attempt to hide their surprise at his looks, made him acutely aware of how different he was and always would be.

The woman studied Stella. He wondered if she was surprised that a woman as beautiful as Stella stood with him. It only took a few seconds before the woman stared at him again. That happened a lot – people were almost physically unable to stop staring at the mess that was his face.

"Hey!" Stella suddenly snapped. "Didn't your mother teach you that it's rude to stare? Go find someone else to ogle. The big guy is with me."

"Excuse me?" the woman said.

"You heard me," Stella said. "Go stare at someone else."

The woman flushed and walked away quickly. Ford's mouth dropped open when Stella yelled, "And don't think I didn't notice you staring at his ass, lady!"

She rolled her eyes as Ford continued to gape at her.

"What?" she asked. "Was I too bitchy? If you hook up with some random woman at the barbeque, I'll be left alone as the awkward third wheel, remember? I'm not letting you ditch me, dude."

"I – she wasn't…"

"She wasn't what? Staring at your ass? Trust me, she was. I thought she was going to start drooling."

"She was staring at my face, Stella, and we both know why," he said. "She's not interested in me."

"Yeah, well, the way she looked at your ass suggested she might be," she said.

Before he could keep arguing, she waved at Jasmine, who approached the ball diamond with her arms loaded with bags of paper plates and plastic utensils. "I'll be right back, Ford. Jasmine needs some help."

* * *

STELLA WALKED QUICKLY TOWARD JASMINE. HER HANDS WERE clenched in fists, and she forced herself to take a deep breath.

She hadn't been lying to Ford. The blonde beauty standing at the end of the picnic table was staring at his ass. She'd taken a nice long look at his entire body, which made Stella's hackles rise for some reason.

Not that she could blame the woman. Ford's body was, in a word, delicious. The loose track pants he wore did nothing to hide the large muscles in his thighs or his mouth-wateringly firm ass, and did he have to wear such a tight t-shirt? The way it clung to his broad chest and abs made her girlie bits tingle.

An utterly ridiculous 'get away from my man' instinct came roaring to life when she saw the look of lust on the woman's face. But how it changed to a look of revulsion when she finally glanced at Ford's face made Stella so angry she wanted to punch the woman.

Calm down, Stella. You and Ford are just friends, remember?

That was true. But didn't friends look out for each other? She had every right to be angry if someone looked at her friend that way. He wasn't a monster, for God's sake. He just looked different.

"Hey, you brought your camera," Jasmine said as Stella took some paper plates from her.

"Yep. Thought I might try to convince a few people to sit for me in between periods of the game," Stella said.

Jasmine laughed. "Innings, Stella. They're called innings in baseball, and there aren't breaks between them."

Stella grinned at her. "I told you I wasn't a baseball player."

"You look awfully cute in your yoga pants, though," Jasmine said.

"Thanks. I almost wore the ones that had 'sexy bitch' written across the ass, but I thought that might give the wrong impression."

Jasmine laughed again as Jimmy waved and jogged toward them.

"Here comes Romeo," Stella said.

Jasmine elbowed her lightly in the side. "Behave, Stella."

* * *

FORD STOOD ON SECOND BASE AND TRIED NOT TO LOOK AT Stella's ass as she bent over and tied her shoe. She had taken off her sweatshirt. She wore a formfitting, navy blue tank top under it, and he was ridiculously distracted by the foreign sight of all that pale skin. For a redhead, she didn't seem to have many freckles, but he wanted to find the ones she did have and lick each one.

After discovering the Myer team was a girl short, Jimmy had volunteered Stella to join their team. They placed her at shortstop, and although she was enthusiastic and tried hard, she was a terrible baseball player. He realized Stella was grinning at him, and he smiled in return. Although he had smiled more in the last two weeks than in his entire lifetime, it still felt stiff and unnatural.

"You'll never make it to third base," she hollered at him.

"You think you're going to stop me?" he taunted as Jimmy came up to bat.

"I'm wearing my running shoes, remember?" She lifted her foot and pointed it at him, giggling when he rolled his eyes.

Jimmy shaded his eyes against the sun before pointing his bat to the left field. There were catcalls and heckling as he winked at Jasmine and shouted, "This home run is for you, Jazzy girl."

"So, wait… you're not going to strike out this time?" she asked sweetly.

He grabbed his chest in a show of mock pain as both teams laughed and heckled him again.

Ignoring them, he held the bat and stepped into position. Jasmine hollered with delight when his bat met the ball with a loud crack and sailed into the left field. He took off for first base as Ford waited where he was. He was confident the outfielder would catch it, and he heard Jimmy's loud curse behind him when the man caught the ball.

Ford immediately took off for third base as the outfielder threw the ball to Stella. Miraculously, she caught it. The second baseman, Devon, shouted, "Tag him, Stella! Tag him!"

She took off like a shot for him. He smiled a little. He could easily dodge her outstretched hand. It would be as easy as taking candy from a –

He grunted in surprise when Stella tackled him. Completely shocked by the feel of her soft body against his, he tripped over his own feet and fell. He twisted onto his back as he fell, terrified he would crush Stella under him. He muttered a curse when he landed on the hard ground with Stella's soft curves pressed intimately against him.

Giggling, Stella straddled him and tapped him lightly on the chest with her glove. "You're out, Ford."

"The ball has to be in your glove," he said.

"What?" She opened her glove and stared blankly at the empty space. "Son of a bitch!"

She glanced around wildly and spotted the ball in the grass above his head. "Dammit!" she shouted as he put his hands on her hips to lift her off him.

He froze when she leaned over him. Her soft, warm, and perfect breasts were smashed delightfully in his face, and his dick immediately hardened.

She snorted in triumph and straightened before touching his chest with the ball she held tightly in her right hand.

"Now you're out!" Her smile faded at the look on his face.

"Ford? Did I hurt you? Oh God, I hurt you. I'm so sorry. I shouldn't have tackled you. Did I crush your ribs? Oh God, I crushed your ribs."

"I'm not hurt," he gritted out.

He wished she would stop talking so animatedly. Her breasts, the ones that only a second ago were planted firmly in his face, now jiggled wildly. His cock was growing harder by the second. Any minute now, she would –

"Oh!" Her eyes widened, and she stared down at where her crotch was pressed against his. He groaned as she made a soft little noise in the back of her throat.

"Ford, I -"

"I'm sorry," he said, pushing her off him. She landed with a hard thump on the ground, and he cursed again when she winced.

"I'm sorry, Stella." He stood up, very aware of the way his dick still strained at his track pants and yanked her to her feet.

"Shit," he said.

Jimmy, Jasmine, Doug, and Devon were all headed toward them. He wondered how fucking weird it would look if he just suddenly bolted from the field. Stella was bright red as she glanced down at his crotch. He had to fight the urge to cover his erection with his hands as the others drew closer. He had just decided to run for it when Stella turned around. She stepped neatly in front of him and used her lush body to hide his obvious erection from the others.

Jimmy grinned at her. "You know this is baseball and not football, right, Stella?"

"You mean I'm not allowed to tackle the opposite team?" she said.

Doug laughed as Jasmine said, "Stella, are you all right?"

"Yes, of course I am," Stella said.

"Are you sure? You look a little flushed."

"I'm not usually much of a sprinter," Stella said. "It's got my heart working overtime."

"Right," Jasmine said as Jimmy grinned at Ford.

"Never thought I'd see the day you'd be knocked down by a woman, big guy."

Ford grunted in reply. His goddamn dick had finally softened, and he could feel shame seeping into him. He was fucking pathetic, and now Stella knew it. He had been a fool to think that he could be friends with a woman like her. Embarrassment coursing through him, he turned and jogged off the field.

* * *

"FORD?"

He groaned inwardly and stared determinedly at the ground as he held a plate of uneaten food in one hand and a beer in the other.

"Ford? Please look at me," Stella said.

He forced his gaze upward. Her cheeks were flushed, but she smiled tentatively at him. "What happened on the field? It's no big deal."

She paused. "Wait – no. I mean, not that *it* isn't big. I'm sure it's nice and big. I mean, it felt big, and I'm sure you have nothing to worry about. You're giant-sized, so obviously your…"

She stared at him in horror before dropping her gaze to the ground. "Oh Jesus, Stella. You fucking idiot!"

She took two deep breaths before meeting his gaze again. "What I'm trying to say and fucking up really bad is that I'm not upset about what happened. It's a perfectly normal reaction, even between friends and -"

"We're not friends," he said.

"What?" she said. "Of course, we're friends. We -"

"No, we're not. I'm sorry if I gave the impression that we were, but I can't be friends with you."

"Why not?"

"I just can't, okay? I need to go – can you let Jimmy know I left?"

He turned and strode away.

* * *

"It's because he wants to bone you, Stella."

"Jimmy!" Jasmine smacked him in the arm and Jimmy shrugged before leaning back in the booth.

"What? I thought it would be helpful to have a man's perspective."

"He doesn't want to bone me, Jimmy," Stella said.

After the barbeque, hurt and upset by what Ford said, Stella agreed to go to the pub with Jimmy, Jasmine, Doug, and Sandra. Doug and Sandra hadn't stayed long, and as soon as they left, Jasmine asked her what was wrong.

She'd told them about the conversation. She said nothing about Ford's erection and lied that her apology was for touching him without his permission.

"I know he's kind of aloof and doesn't like to be touched," she said, "but I didn't think it would mean that he would dump me as a friend."

Jimmy took a drink of beer. "He doesn't want to be friends because he wants to bang you, Stella."

"You're not helping, Jimmy," Jasmine said.

"I am," he insisted. "Listen, I've worked with Ford for three fucking years and never once seen the guy smile. Not once. Then he's hanging out with Stella, and suddenly, he's

Mr. Guy Smiley. He's had a crush on you since you started working upstairs, Stella."

"No, he doesn't," Stella said. "He's had plenty of opportunities to ask me out, and he hasn't. Plus, he spends most of our lunches lecturing me about my eating habits."

"Whatever, dude. The guy has it bad for you. He hasn't asked you out because he thinks his ugly mug has no chance with a girl like you."

"Don't call him ugly," Stella said. "He isn't ugly."

Jasmine and Jimmy exchanged looks, and Stella glared at them. "He isn't ugly. He's unique looking."

"The point I'm trying to make," Jimmy said, "is that he has a crush on you, and you're probably the first girl who's ever given him the time of day. Then you point out that you guys are *friends,* and his dream of banging you dies. No guy likes to hear 'Hey, we're friends' from the girl he wants to have a go at. Of course, he's upset. He probably thought this was his only chance to lose his virginity."

"He told you he was a virgin?" Jasmine asked.

"Shit, no. But c'mon, we all know the guy is. No woman would sleep with him."

Jasmine frowned at him and shifted away. "You're being really cruel about someone who is supposed to be your friend."

"No," Jimmy said, "I'm being truthful, and there's a difference. Do I wish Ford would get laid? Hell, yes. I feel bad for the guy, and he's my friend. But can you honestly tell me that you would sleep with him, Jasmine?"

She hesitated, and he said, "See, you know I'm right."

"He has a great body," Jasmine said. "Just because I don't want to sleep with him doesn't mean there aren't women out there who do."

"It's not just his looks, Jasmine. The guy is an introvert. We've been friends for three years, and I barely know anything about him. Women like men to open up about their feelings, and Ford won't say two words to anyone."

"Do you want to date him, Stella?" Jasmine said.

"If he asked me out, I wouldn't say no," Stella said.

Jasmine turned to Jimmy. "Tell him that on Monday, Jimmy."

"Will do, Jazzy girl," Jimmy said.

CHAPTER 4

S tella pressed the lobby button and leaned against the elevator wall. She was tired and hungry and anxious to be home. Unfortunately, her car started making a weird clicking noise last week, and she dropped it off at the mechanic this morning. She would be taking the bus home and glanced down at her shoes with a small grimace. She really should have brought her running shoes to change into.

The elevator moved smoothly downward, and she mentally prepared herself not to look at the security desk in the lobby. It had been a month since the barbeque, and Ford hadn't spoken a single word to her. He didn't look at her when she walked past in the morning or at the end of the day, and he didn't go to the atrium for lunch anymore.

A week after the barbeque, she pestered Jasmine to find out if Jimmy told Ford she would go out with him if he asked. Jasmine finally admitted that Jimmy had spoken to him, but Ford wasn't interested in dating her.

At Stella's crushed look, Jasmine tried to comfort her. "Jimmy thinks he's lying, Stella."

She'd shrugged and forced herself to smile. "It's fine. But I wish we could return to being friends, at least."

She straightened her skirt as the elevator slowed to a stop. The damn thing was too tight. She had comforted herself with ice cream for too many nights in the last month and silently berated herself.

So Ford isn't interested in you – get over it. Not all guys like chubby girls. Don't take it personally, for God's sake.

If she was being honest, she was upset by Ford's lack of interest in her but not that surprised. Being plus-sized had always limited her dating options. Just because Ford didn't have movie star looks didn't mean that he should automatically settle for a fat girl if he didn't like a little extra cushion on a girl. She would be irritated and upset with him if he did.

He got an erection, remember?

Yeah, she remembered. But she had kind of shoved her tits in his face. Even if he wasn't attracted to her – guys liked tits.

The loss of their budding friendship bothered her the most and sent her diving into a bowl of Rocky Road every night. She'd enjoyed their lunches together even if she did most of the talking, and she'd been sure he enjoyed them, too. He'd even started to open up a bit more. Well, if describing in detail what he cooked for dinner the night before was opening up. Now that their daily lunch ritual was over, she realized how much she looked forward to them.

The elevator doors slid open, and she zipped up her jacket. The weather had turned from cool to cold during the last two days. She started across the lobby without glancing at the security desk. Most likely, Ford would be gone, and it would be Doug sitting at the desk. Ford worked the day shift, and they usually finished work around the same time, but she had worked late tonight. Still, she didn't want to risk glancing over and seeing the top of his head as he stared fixedly at the desk, so she kept her eyes averted.

She stepped outside and immediately shivered. She wished she had thought to bring gloves. It rained for most of the day and turned to freezing rain late in the afternoon. The sidewalk was icy as hell, and she walked gingerly on her too-high heels toward the bus stop.

It was dark with a cold wind. Thanks to the late hour, the street was eerily empty. No cars were idling at the light, and not a single person walked down the sidewalk. The wind blew in her face, and she winced as she skirted around the giant puddle in front of the bus stop. It was a twenty-minute wait until the next bus, but at least this stop had a shelter. She might not freeze to death if she –

"Give me your purse, lady."

She stared dumbly at the man standing in the bus shelter. He was tall with wide shoulders and pale skin. He picked absently at the scabs on his face as he stared at her.

"I'm sorry?" she said.

"Your purse!" he snapped. "Give me your fucking purse."

She glanced at her purse slung over her shoulder. "No."

"Bitch, give me your fucking purse, or I swear to God, I will fuck you up!" the man snarled.

"Get away from me," she said as she backed away. Adrenaline flooded her veins, making her pulse race and her legs tremble. The man lunged forward and grabbed the strap of her purse. She held it grimly and tried to break away.

"You stupid bitch!" he shouted. She screamed shrilly as he grabbed her arm and squeezed it viciously.

"Shut up!" he shouted again.

She twisted violently in his grip, refusing to give up her hold on her purse. It dangled between them as they engaged in a game of tug of war until, finally, with a growl of anger, he punched her in the side of the face. Pain shot through her, and she let go of her purse. He shoved her in the chest, and she stumbled back, her right ankle twisting painfully. She screamed again as she twisted around and tumbled to the ground, falling face-first into the large puddle behind her. Ice-cold water soaked through her thin jacket and into her shirt and skirt. She moaned in fear when the man leaned over her and flipped her onto her back.

"If you had just given me your goddamn purse, I wouldn't have to -"

There was an inarticulate roar of rage, and the man was ripped away from her. She watched numbly as Ford wrapped his hand around the man's neck and lifted him as easily as a ragdoll. He threw him against the glass wall of the bus shelter and tightened his hand around the man's throat. The man choked and flailed in his harsh grip, clutching weakly at Ford's arms as Ford bared his teeth at him.

"I'll fucking kill you for touching her. Do you hear me, you miserable piece of shit?"

A hand wrapped around her arm, and she gasped in fear as Doug hauled her to her feet. "Stella? Are you okay?"

"I – yeah, I think so," she said. "Ford. I want Ford."

Doug turned toward Ford, his eyes widening. "Ford, let him go! You're killing him!"

Ford ignored him and squeezed harder. The man was going limp. Terrified that Ford really would kill him, Stella shouted, "Ford, stop! Please!"

At the sound of her voice, he dropped the man to the ground and stalked toward her. His face was a mask of pure fury, but his touch was gentle when he traced his fingers across her cheek. "Are you all right?"

"I'm okay," she said as he put one large arm around her waist and drew her against him.

"I'm getting you wet," she said through numb lips.

"Did he hurt you?" Ford scanned her face anxiously.

"I – he punched me in the face, but I'm okay."

Another look of rage flickered across his face, and she threw her arms around his shoulders when he started to pull away. "Please don't, Ford. Don't leave me."

Doug touched her arm. "You need to go to the hospital, Stella."

"No, I don't. I'm okay."

"Call the cops, Doug," Ford said as he stared at Stella's face. "Tell them there's been an attempted mugging and -"

"Shit!" Doug said.

"What?"

"He's fucking gone."

Ford turned, still holding her firmly against his chest. He muttered a curse and pushed away from Stella. "He can't have gotten far. I'll find him and -"

Fear shot through Stella. She pressed up against him, wrapping her arms around his waist again. "Ford, don't leave me! Please."

Doug scooped up her purse as Ford touched her cheek with infinite gentleness. He picked her up and carried her toward the office.

* * *

"WELL, IT SOUNDS LIKE IT'S THE SAME GUY WHO MUGGED three people last week."

"Are you fucking kidding me?" Ford glared at the cop standing in front of him. "Why the fuck haven't you found him yet? Do you know how to do your fucking job?"

"Ford, don't," Stella said. She had removed her wet clothes and wore Ford's security uniform shirt. It was way too big, and fell past her knees. She winced when the paramedic pressed against her cheekbone.

"I don't think anything's broken," he said as he removed

his gloves, "but we can take you to the hospital for an X-ray to be certain."

She shook her head and pressed the icepack against her cheek again. "No, I'm fine."

"Stella, you need to go to the hospital," Ford said.

"I don't want to. I'm fine – it's not broken," she said.

The cop crouched in front of Stella. "We've got your description of him. You may have to come in to identify him via line-up when we find him, okay?"

She nodded, and he patted her arm. "I have your contact information, and I'll call when we catch him. I would advise that you don't wait at the bus stop by yourself after dark any -"

"She won't be," Ford said. "She's not going anywhere by herself again."

The cop eyed him before nodding. The paramedics finished repacking their supplies, shook Stella's hand, and left.

"You have my card, Ms. Johnson. Call me if you have any questions or concerns," the officer said. Doug followed the cop out of the office and past the security desk as Ford crouched in front of Stella.

"I wish you would go to the hospital, Stella."

"I don't want to," she said. "I just want to go home."

"I'll drive you home."

"Thank you."

He helped her to stand and quickly bundled her into his coat before throwing her wet jacket and clothes into a bag.

"You'll be too cold," she said as she stared at his thin white t-shirt.

"I'll be fine."

Doug popped his head into the office. "Ford, are you taking Stella home?"

"Yes."

"Okay. Good night, Stella. I'm sorry about what happened."

"Thanks, Doug."

She took a step, wincing when it made her ankle throb dully. She twitched in surprise when Ford scooped her up.

He carried her toward the exit at the back of the building, and she patted his shoulder. "Put me down. You'll break your back if you have to carry my heavy ass to your car."

He snorted. "You're not heavy."

"Kind but ridiculously inaccurate," she mumbled. She was suddenly very tired and wanted to bury her face in Ford's warm neck and forget the entire night.

As if he had read her mind, his large hand cupped the back of her neck and guided her head down. She pushed her face into his throat and clung to him as he walked outside to the parking lot behind the building. He carried her to his truck and helped her into the seat, buckling the seatbelt around her. As he started the truck and drove out of the parking lot, she recited her address and closed her eyes.

* * *

"You don't have to carry me -"

She gave up with a soft sigh as Ford lifted her out of the truck and slammed the door shut with his foot. He carried her toward her townhouse. The curtains in the townhouse to the left twitched, and Stella knew that Mrs. Morrison was studying them. The old woman was retired and had nothing better to do than spy on her neighbours. By tomorrow night at this time, the entire complex would know that Stella had been carried into her house by a giant.

Ford took the keys from her hand and opened the door before setting her down in the hallway. She smiled tiredly at him and shrugged out of his jacket. "Thank you for the ride home. I'll wash your shirt and return it to you on Monday, okay?"

"What are you going to do now?" he asked.

"Have a ridiculously hot shower, grab the crowbar from the basement, and sit terrified on the couch until the sun rises?" She was only half-joking.

Ford took off his shoes. "Go get in the shower. I'll make you something to eat."

"Ford, no," she said. "You don't have to do that. I was kidding."

"You weren't, and we both know it."

"Ford…"

She did want him to stay. The thought of being alone right now scared her. She could call her brother - he'd stay with her. Hell, she could go to her sister's or her parents' place and spend the night. But she didn't want that. She wanted to be home, and she wanted Ford to stay.

"Do you need help upstairs?" Ford asked.

She limped her way to the staircase. "No, my ankle is feeling a little better. I – thank you."

"You're welcome."

* * *

"THAT SMELLS GOOD." SHE SMILED AT HIM AS HE CARRIED A tray into her small living room. She was sitting on the couch with her foot propped up on the ottoman and a bag of frozen peas on her ankle. She set the icepack she was holding to her face on the arm of the couch.

Ford set the tray on the cushion beside her and studied her face. "You'll have a bruise."

"Yeah." She inhaled the good smells drifting from the bowl on the tray. Her stomach growled, and a small smile crossed Ford's face.

"I made you some soup, figured it might hurt to chew."

"Thanks, Ford."

He set the tray on her lap, and she tasted the soup as he left and returned with his own bowl of steaming soup. He sat in the chair beside the sofa, and they ate silently.

"You should eat some more," he said when she returned the half-full bowl to the tray.

"I'm full," she said.

He frowned but didn't argue as he took the tray and carried it to the kitchen. When he returned, she held the ice pack to her face with her eyes closed. He sat down, and without opening her eyes, she said, "Why can't we be friends?"

"I'm sorry?"

She could tell he was stalling. "At the barbeque, you said you couldn't be friends with me."

"I didn't mean it," he said.

She opened her eyes and stared at him. "Then why did you say it?"

"I don't know. I was embarrassed, I guess."

"There's nothing to be embarrassed about. I told you it was a normal reaction."

"Yeah." He stared at his hands. "I want to be friends with you."

He emphasized the word 'friends,' and she ignored the ripple of dismay that went through her.

"I want that too. I've missed our lunches."

"I have too," he admitted.

She smiled at him before glancing at the clock. "It's getting late. You should probably go home and get some sleep."

* * *

43

FORD DIDN'T WANT TO LEAVE. NOT WHEN STELLA LOOKED tired and afraid. She was being brave, but he knew what happened tonight scared her.

"I can stay the night," he said, blushing furiously. "I mean – I know you're scared, and I don't mind staying."

"I am scared," she said, "and I hate that I am."

He gave her knee two quick pats. "I can teach you some self-defense moves."

"Really?"

"Yes. If you want."

"I do." She smiled at him and then winced and rubbed her cheek. "Thanks, I appreciate that."

"Why were you taking the bus anyway?"

"My car is in the shop. Why were you working so late?"

"I had some stuff to finish up."

That was a lie. He stayed late because Stella hadn't come downstairs yet, and he wanted one last glimpse of her before the weekend.

"How did you know I was in trouble?"

"I heard you screaming," he said. A small shudder went through him. He'd been walking toward the front doors, curious why Stella hadn't gone out the back toward the parking lot like usual. He would never have heard her scream if he hadn't decided to check and stayed where he was behind the security desk.

"When do you get your car back?" he said.

She shrugged. "Tuesday, I think. They're pretty busy."

"I'll pick you up Monday morning for work and drive you home."

"You don't have to do that. I'm sure it will be fine, and I -"

"I'm picking you up and driving you home," he said. "It's what friends do, right?"

"Yes," she said. "You don't have to stay the night."

"I don't mind."

"My second bedroom is my studio. I don't have an extra bed," she said.

"I can sleep on the couch."

She laughed and then winced before placing the ice pack on her face. "You won't get any sleep. The couch is too short for you."

"I'm staying, Stella," he said.

She gave his hand a quick squeeze. "Thank you."

CHAPTER 5

The nightmare woke her at two. She lurched upward, gasping and shaking with tears sliding down her cheeks. She pressed her hand against her chest, feeling the runaway beat of her heart as she climbed out of the bed.

She stumbled to the bathroom and stared at herself in the mirror. "You're okay, Stella. You're okay. Ford's here, you're safe."

Her hands shaking, she flipped off the light and limped back to her bed. She paused before leaving the bedroom and limping silently down the stairs. She was getting a drink of water, she told herself. She certainly wasn't hoping that Ford would be awake.

She crept by the couch. Ford was a large, blanket-covered lump, and she made an undignified shriek when he sat up.

"Stella? What's wrong?"

"N-nothing," she said. "I was getting a drink of water. I'm sorry. I didn't mean to wake you."

He threw back the blanket, and she stared up at him when he stood in front of her. He touched her shoulder gingerly. "You're shaking."

"I had a bad dream," she said and then embarrassed herself by bursting into tears.

"Don't cry, Stella," Ford said, patting her back timidly.

She pushed herself up against him, wrapping her arms around his waist and burying her face in his broad chest. He stiffened and then led her to the couch. She refused to let him go, and they collapsed awkwardly onto the couch together.

"I'm sorry," she said.

"Don't be," he said. "You had a scary experience earlier, and it's natural that you -"

Desperate for comfort and not caring how it looked, Stella crawled into his lap and buried her face in his thick neck. He rubbed her back through her thin shirt.

"I hate being so afraid and being such a baby."

"You're not being a baby."

"I am," she said.

Ford didn't reply but rubbed her back until her trembling stopped.

"Better?" he said

She nodded but clung to him when he tried to move her off his lap. "I don't want to be alone," she said.

"You should crawl back into bed and get some sleep," he said.

"No way," she said. "I'm staying here with you." Feeling like a whiny baby but not giving a shit, she continued to cling to him. She needed to be with Ford tonight. He made her feel safe.

* * *

STELLA FELT SO GOOD SITTING IN HIS LAP, AND IF HE HADN'T been so worried about her, he'd have a massive erection right now.

48

She needed sleep, though. He could see the weariness on her face.

"Let me stay with you," she said.

"The couch isn't big enough for both of us."

"Then come upstairs with me." She stared pleadingly at him.

"I can't, Stella."

Ford could feel sweat on his forehead at just the thought of being in Stella's bed. What would it be like to stretch out next to her and have her warm curves pressed against him all night? He wouldn't be able to stop himself from touching her. He knew that without a doubt. The disgust on her face when he made a move on her would destroy him.

"Please, Ford. I can't – I can't go upstairs by myself," she said.

Her pleading and the raw fear in her eyes did him in. "Okay."

"Thank you." She kissed his cheek and slid from his lap. Holding tightly to his hand, she led him up the stairs and into her room.

He eyed her bed with something close to panic. It was a double, and with Stella's curves and his wide body, there was no way he could avoid touching her.

She climbed into bed and patted the spot next to her. "Lie down."

He stretched out on the very edge of the bed, groaning inwardly when Stella crowded up against him and put her arm around his waist. He lifted his arm, and she nosed under it before resting her head on his bare chest and sighing happily.

"Thank you."

"You're welcome, Stella."

He stared at the ceiling as Stella squirmed a little closer. Her hair was everywhere, wrapped around his arm and brushing against his ribcage. Fuck, she smelled good. His dick was hardening, and he hoped desperately she wouldn't notice the lump against the quilt.

He closed his eyes and thought about his family, their disgust and anger at his very existence. He thought about Diana and how she had made him turn his face away when they were in bed together. Shame swept through him, erasing his desire and his erection. He didn't flinch when Stella squirmed even closer. She was already half-asleep.

He resisted the urge to stroke her flame-coloured hair and ignored the feel of her clearly bra-less breasts pushing against his side. She told Jimmy she would go out with him, but he knew it was just pity on her part.

He and Stella were friends, and that's all they would ever be.

* * *

SLEEPING WITH FORD WAS AMAZING, STELLA DECIDED BEFORE even opening her eyes. She could feel the morning light on her face, and she smiled a little when Ford snored quietly behind her. When she fell asleep last night, Ford was lying on his back, and she was curled up against him. At some point, they had turned on their sides.

She enjoyed both being the little spoon to Ford's big – hell, massive – spoon and the feel of his erection against her ass. She rubbed against it experimentally, another smile crossing her face when Ford's hand moved from her waist to her breast in response. He cupped her breast and squeezed gently.

She opened her eyes and stared at her chest. Ford's hand was so big that her boobs looked almost normal sized in his grip. His hand was warm, and she wished she could feel it against her bare skin. Maybe she could hike up her shirt and pretend it had ridden up in her sleep. She grabbed the front of her t-shirt and tugged it. To her disappointment, Ford released her breast and rolled onto his back.

She turned over and studied him in the light, resisting the urge to climb out of bed and grab her camera. She wouldn't take his picture without his permission, but maybe she could convince him to sit for her before he left.

She let her gaze drift down his naked chest. The quilt and sheet were bunched around his waist, and she touched his chest, covered in the perfect amount of dark hair. She ran one finger down the visible muscles in his abdomen.

One, two, three, four, five, six, she counted silently. She wasn't surprised by Ford's six pack, but she was a little surprised by her almost irresistible urge to trace each ab muscle with her tongue. She touched the line of hair below his navel, her eyes widening when she caught sight of the bulge against the quilt.

Don't, Stella! How would you like it if Ford stared at and groped you while you were sleeping?

Fuck, she should be so lucky.

She cast a quick, guilty look at Ford's face before gently easing back the quilt to the middle of his thighs. He was wearing a pair of boxer shorts, and she studied how the material tented before reaching for the elastic waistband.

Stella! Don't you dare! Don't even think about it!

The screeching of her inner voice returned a smidge of her sanity, and she clenched her hands together, still studying the front of Ford's boxer shorts. Lust was rolling through her belly, hardening her nipples and dampening the crotch of her panties as she pictured herself on her knees in front of Ford and that maybe – *probably* – giant dick of his. If Jimmy was right and Ford was a virgin, he had most likely never gotten a blow job before. Her mouth watered at the thought of being the first woman to show Ford how good it would feel.

And just like that, her fingers traced the waistband of his boxers again.

She snatched them back in a hurry when Ford's hips rocked forward the tiniest bit. She stared at him, her heart melting a little at the combination of sleepiness and desire on his face as he studied her.

"Stella?" he rasped. "What's wrong?"

"Nothing," she said. "I was... I mean... You have an amazing body, and I really want to look at your dick."

Fucking hell, Stella!

She was about to stammer out an apology when Ford yawned before his eyes fluttered shut. "Sure, go ahead."

She nearly fell off the bed. Was Ford serious? She needed to make certain, but instead she reached out, her hand trembling wildly, and carefully pulled the waistband of his boxers away from his body. She peeked down the front of his boxers, and her mouth dropped open.

"Holy mother of god," she whispered.

She hadn't slept with a lot of men, four to be exact, but she'd watched her fair share of porn. Ford's dick would make a porn star feel inadequate. She licked her lips and took another long look. She wanted to touch it, wanted to feel that hard steel encased in velvet skin as Ford moaned and panted and begged for her mouth.

Stella! Enough, you fucking creeper! What the hell are you doing? Ford wants to be just friends, remember? He said you could look because he's half-asleep or something. What do you think will happen if you grope his junk like a sexual predator? If you're lucky, he'll just never talk to you again instead of charging you with sexual harassment.

Her eyes widened, and she let go of his waistband and scrambled from the bed. What the hell was she doing? She had touched Ford, had looked down his goddamn boxers like the world's biggest pervert when Ford undoubtedly was half asleep and not even aware of what he said. He saved her life last night, and she was repaying him by trying to molest him.

"Stella, you fucking idiot!" She slapped herself on the forehead.

"Stella? What's wrong?" Ford sat up and stared anxiously at her. "Are you okay?"

"Yes, I'm fine."

To her horror, her eyes dropped to his crotch. His erection still strained against his boxers, and he followed her gaze. He cursed and snatched up the quilt. "Sorry. I'll leave now."

His face was bright red, and he looked wide awake now with that sleepy desire replaced by pure misery. Before he could slide from the bed, she said, "No, don't leave. It's fine, really. Also, I looked down your shorts because I'm a pervert. I'm sorry. I'll understand if you don't want to be friends anymore, but I swear I'm not normally like this. I think that guy gave me brain damage last night when he punched me. I'm not, like, a sexual predator or anything like that. Honestly."

"I said you could look," Ford said, his cheeks still a bright red.

"I'm pretty sure you were half asleep and not really aware of what you were agreeing to," she said. "Am I wrong?"

He just shrugged, and the heavy silence between them made panic flood through her. Desperate to fix what she'd done, she blurted, "I'll show you mine!"

He blinked at her. "You'll show me your what?"

"My girlie bits. I've seen your boy bits, so it's only fair you see my girl bits, right? Then we'll be even Steven, yeah?" Her voice was bordering on hysteria.

Stella! Get it together, girl!

"What do you think?" she said. "Ford? Say something, please."

"I can't look at – I mean, it's not…"

His gaze dropped to her crotch, and new colour appeared in his cheeks.

"I don't mind," she babbled as she moved toward him. "In fact, I insist. I would feel much better about what I did if you let me show you. Please, I don't want this to ruin our friendship again. Okay?"

"Stella, I…" He stared at her in panic and leaned back in the bed as she stood before him and grabbed the waistband of her sleep shorts.

"Oh my God," she said as fresh embarrassment flooded through her. "What the hell am I doing?"

She gave him a horrified look. "I am so sorry. I'll hide in the kitchen until you leave. I… thank you again for saving me last night, and it was, um, really nice being your friend."

She turned and hurried toward the door, tears pricking at her eyes as she berated herself inwardly.

"Stella, show me."

His low voice stopped her in her tracks. She pivoted slowly, staring uncertainly at him. "What did you say?"

He was sitting on the side of the bed with his hands clenched in tight fists. "I'm not upset with you, and we're still friends, but if it makes you feel better about what you did, show me."

"It would," she said. "It really would."

He nodded, and she moved across the room to stand before him. He stared at her for a long moment before lowering his gaze. She took a deep breath, stepped between his legs, and pulled the waistband of her shorts and panties away from her body. He peered down her shorts and inhaled sharply.

She stood silently, staring at the top of his dark head as he continued to look. He lifted one badly trembling hand and held it just above her open waistband. Her breath caught in her throat, and she leaned forward a little. Her lust was back, overpowering her shame and embarrassment. She could think of nothing but how it would feel to have Ford's hand between her legs.

Touch me, Ford. Please touch me.

He suddenly dropped his hand back to the bed and clutched the quilt. "Go downstairs. I'll be down in a minute."

His voice was strangled, and she hesitated. "Ford, I -"

"Go, Stella! Please!"

She let go of her waistband with a snap and hurried to the bedroom door. "I'll make us some breakfast, okay?"

"Sure." His eyes were closed, and she could see his cock straining at his boxers.

"Okay, see you in a few minutes," she whispered, booking it from the bedroom.

* * *

"You're not eating, Ford."

Ford stared blankly at his plate of food, only dimly aware of Stella's soft voice. He was deep in a fantasy that involved a naked Stella lying on the kitchen table and begging him to bury his face in her pussy.

His cock was hard as a rock, and he couldn't get the image of Stella's pussy out of his head. He hadn't seen much, just a glorious patch of red hair, a line of three perfect freckles just above that red hair, and a hint of her pink lips, but his imagination was in overdrive.

Why the hell had he asked her to show him? Why? It hadn't upset him that Stella took a look at his junk. Hell, in a weird way, he was flattered by it. But then she started babbling about showing him hers, and what little blood was left in his head had completely drained to his dick.

He had agreed to play what amounted to an X-rated version of Show and Tell because he wanted Stella, but now, he regretted it. He would never get the image of her pussy out of his head. Not even if he lived to be a hundred.

Stella's soft hand touched his, and he raised his head. "I'm not hungry for food, Stella."

"What are you hungry for?" she asked with an innocent smile.

"Your pussy."

Her cheeks flushed, and she gave him a sweet look of need. "If you eat my pussy, it's only fair that I suck your cock, right?"

His balls tightened, and it was all he could do not to reach down and stroke his dick. Diana had taught him many things, but she had never gone down on him. She had refused, even after he offered to –

His cheeks burned, and he pushed the memory out of his head. He was deeply ashamed of the way he had begged and even more ashamed of what he offered her to do it, but he could do nothing about it. It happened, and he had to live with it.

"Ford?"

Stella had left her seat and was already kneeling in front of him. He reached down and touched a lock of her hair, feeling the softness against his fingertips as she reached for the waistband of his boxers.

"Can I suck your cock, Ford? Please?"

"Yes," he said hoarsely. "Yes, Stella."

She smiled happily at him, and he lifted his ass from the chair so she could drag his boxers down his thighs. She licked her lips, and he cupped the back of her head and guided her mouth toward his cock. Her lips parted, and he groaned at the feel of her warm breath on the head of his cock.

"Ford?"

He jerked himself out of his sex fantasy and stared blankly at Stella. She was sitting at the far end of the kitchen table, staring worriedly at him. He cleared his throat as she said, "I've ruined everything, haven't I?"

"No, of course not."

"I have," she said miserably before staring at the food on her plate. She had cooked a big breakfast, eggs, oatmeal, pancakes, and toast, but her food was untouched.

"I'm sorry," she said.

"You have nothing to be sorry about," he said. "Even Steven, remember?"

"Right," she said.

"I mean it. It's no big deal."

She flushed, and he smiled hesitantly at her. "You know what I mean."

"I'm not a pervert, I swear," she said.

"I know you're not," he said. "Listen, we'll forget what happened this morning, okay?"

"Okay," she said.

"What are your plans for the weekend?" He poured some syrup on his pancakes. He shoved the image from his brain of pouring the syrup on Stella's naked breasts and licking her clean and forced himself to take a bite of pancakes. He didn't have much of an appetite. His lust for Stella had taken it clean away, but he didn't want her feeling any worse than she already did.

"I'm having lunch with my sister and her kids," she said before poking at her egg with the tip of her fork. "What about you?"

"Working out and then maybe going to a movie."

"What movie?"

"I haven't decided yet."

"I want to see that new horror film. It came out last week-end," Stella said before dropping her fork and sipping her coffee.

"You like horror movies?"

She nodded, a small smile crossing her face. "Yeah, always have. I used to make my brother stay up late with me when we were teens and have horror marathons. Of course, Brandon is twenty-four now and still sleeps with a night light – which he blames me for entirely."

He laughed, and she smiled hesitantly at him. "He refuses to watch horror movies with me now. He says he's trau-matized."

He ate another forkful of pancakes as she said, "Do you like horror movies?"

"I'll watch just about anything," he said. "Did you want to go to the movies with me later? I'll watch the horror movie with you if you want."

"I'd like that," she said. "If you don't mind hanging out with me again?"

"Of course, I don't," he said. "We're friends, right?"

"Right," she said.

He frowned at the look on her face. "What?"

"Nothing. Do you want some more food?"

He shook his head and glanced at his watch. "I should probably get going. I'll swing by and pick you up around six-thirty if that works. We could go to the early show and grab a bite to eat afterward."

"It's a plan," she said and smiled with relief at him.

He returned her smile as an image of Stella giving him a blow job in the dark theatre went through his head.

Fuck, he was in so much trouble.

CHAPTER 6

"Stella, pay attention."

"I'm paying attention," she lied.

She shifted a little, and Ford loosened his grip around her throat. She decided it probably made her the biggest pervert on earth to be turned on by a chokehold. She'd spent the last two weeks coming to Ford's house every few days to learn self-defense moves. With every lesson, it was growing harder and harder to ignore her lust.

Telling herself to behave, she stepped back until she was pressed against Ford's hard body. Her ass brushed against his crotch, and she ignored her trickle of disappointment. Why would Ford have an erection? He didn't find her attractive and was trying to teach her self-defense moves, not cop a feel.

"What do you do now?" Ford asked.

She gripped his forearm and pretended to stomp on the top of his foot before shifting her body to the side. She swung her fist back, stopping just short of his crotch, and grinned up at him.

"Shot to the nuts, and the big boy goes down."

He rolled his eyes. "As soon as your attacker releases you, what do you do?"

"Run like hell," she said.

"Good." He stepped away from her. "We'll keep practicing for another month or so, okay?"

"Sure," she said before collapsing on the couch. She smiled at Ford when he sat next to her. She studied his large thigh. It was brushing against hers, and she casually let her legs fall open so that her thigh pressed more intimately against his. He immediately stood, and she sighed inwardly. God, she constantly made a fool of herself with him.

Just friends, Stella. Just friends.

Right, just friends.

"Are you hungry?" Ford headed into the kitchen before she could reply. She followed him to the kitchen and sat at the table. He took the lid off the pot on the stove and stirred the contents.

"That smells good."

"I wasn't sure if you liked chili," he said.

"I do."

"This is vegetarian chili," he said as he tasted a spoonful.

"Vegetarian? I thought you were a meat eater," Stella said.

He shrugged. "I do a couple of vegetarian meals a week."

"Oh," she said.

"You don't like vegetarian chili?"

"Uh, yeah, I like it," she said. "Are there a lot of beans in it?"

He nodded, and she forced herself to smile. "Great."

When he turned away, she dropped her head into her hands. Lots of beans – awesome. She'd have to make a quick exit after dinner. If Ford didn't find her attractive now, the farting she would undoubtedly do from eating the chili wouldn't help change his mind.

"Stella? You okay?"

She raised her head and smiled at him. "Yes. I wanted to ask you something, though."

"What's that?"

"Will you sit for me in my studio?"

He grimaced and bit at his bottom lip. "You don't want to take pictures of my ugly mug, Stella."

She frowned at him. "Don't call yourself ugly, and yes, I do."

"Why?"

"Because I like the way you look," she said.

He flushed bright red and stirred the chili again. "I'm not comfortable with having my picture taken."

"I won't show them to anyone else, I promise. If you hate them, I'll delete them. "

"Can I think about it?"

"Sure. Hey, do you want to drive together tomorrow night?"

"Uh, I wasn't going to go," he said.

"Why not? You told me you love playing pool."

"It's been a long week, and I'm tired."

"Tomorrow is Friday. You can sleep in the next day," Stella said. "I already told Jasmine and Jimmy I would meet them at the pool hall. It won't be any fun if you don't come, too."

"Yeah, okay. I'll go."

"Good. It'll be fun. You'll see."

"Right," he said. "I have a few errands to run after work, so can I meet you there?"

She stared suspiciously at him. "You're not doing that thing where a person says they'll go and then bails last minute, are you?"

"No. I'll be there."

She relaxed and smiled at him. "Awesome. Maybe after pool, you and I can go for coffee?"

You're such a dork!

She ignored her inner voice as Ford said, "Sure."

* * *

FORD OPENED THE DOOR AND STEPPED INTO THE POOL HALL. He searched for Stella and the others, ignoring the looks of the people closest to the door. He didn't particularly want to be here but couldn't resist Stella's plea to join them. Hell, he couldn't resist Stella, period.

She came to his house at least twice a week to practice her self-defense moves and have dinner with him. He was happy to teach her how to protect herself, but being that close to her was hell. It was sheer willpower alone that kept his dick from hardening every time her ass brushed against him. But that was getting more and more difficult with every lesson.

How long will you keep doing this, Ford? Will you really be happy being Stella's friend for the rest of your life? What happens when she starts dating someone? Gets married? You're already halfway to being in love with her.

He tuned out his inner voice and scanned the pool hall again. A group of three women stood just to his left, and one of them whispered something to the others before staring at him. All three burst into peals of laughter, and he looked away.

"Ford! Ford, over here!"

Stella was waving at him, and his heart thudded heavily as he approached the pool table. Jimmy and Jasmine waved at him as Stella gave him a friendly hug. Her soft breasts pressed against his chest, and, God, her hair smelled so good. He gritted his teeth and quickly stepped away before he embarrassed himself.

Her smile faltered, and she crossed her arms over her chest. "Thanks for coming."

"I said I would," he said.

"I know," she said. "Are you ready to play pool?"

He nodded, and she hooked her arm around his in a friendly way. "Awesome. We're playing girls against guys, so be prepared to get your ass kicked by Jasmine and me."

He laughed, and she poked him playfully in the side. "I'm not joking. I'm a total pool shark."

She grabbed a pool cue before pointing it at Jimmy. "Rack 'em up, Jimmy."

* * *

"Four beers, please," Ford said to the bartender.

The man nodded and scanned his face briefly before turning away. Ford drummed his fingers on the bar as he waited. He twitched when he felt the hand on his shoulder. He turned to see a pretty, slender blonde woman standing next to him. She had dark brown eyes, and a thick layer of makeup covered her porcelain skin.

"Hey there, big guy." Her gaze wandered over his face before dropping to his chest. She let her hand run down the thick muscles in his upper arm. "My name's Cassie. What's yours?"

"Uh, Ford."

"It's nice to meet you, uh, Ford," she said teasingly.

"Nice to meet you too," he mumbled as the bartender set the beers before him. Ford handed him some cash and waved off the change.

"I was watching you play pool. You're pretty good," Cassie said.

"Thanks."

"My friends and I wanted to play pool, but all the tables

are full," she pouted. "Do you think we could join you and your girlfriend?"

She glanced at Stella, who was laughing at something Jimmy was saying.

"Uh, she's not my girlfriend. We're just friends," Ford said.

"Really?" Cassie said. "Well, what do you say? Can we join you?"

He cleared his throat and glanced at her two friends. "Um…"

"Pretty please." Cassie leaned against him, her breasts pressing against his arm. He shifted away from her as she pouted again. "Please, Ford. We really want to play pool."

"Uh, sure, okay."

"Thank you so much!" She tried to hug him, and he stepped back, nearly tripping over his feet.

She didn't seem to notice and picked up two of the beers. "Here, let me help you carry these."

Feeling anxious and unsettled, Ford followed Cassie and her friends to the pool table.

* * *

"Is it just me, or does that Cassie chick totally want to bang Ford?" Jasmine said into Stella's ear.

Stella nodded. "Yeah."

"Well, good for Ford," Jasmine said.

"Yeah," Stella repeated.

"Are you okay with that?"

"Why wouldn't I be? Ford and I are just friends."

"Right," Jasmine said.

They watched as Cassie leaned over the pool table and smiled at Ford. "Am I doing this right, Ford?"

He nodded and eased away from the pool table as she

said, "I don't think I'm holding the pool cue right. Can you help me?"

Ford gave Stella a quick look, and she forced herself to smile at him. Without speaking, he helped Cassie reposition the pool cue.

"She just rubbed her ass against his crotch!" Stella said in an outraged whisper.

"Thought you didn't care," Jasmine said.

Stella scowled at her, and Jasmine squeezed her arm. "Sorry. I don't think you need to worry. Ford doesn't seem to be all that interested in her. Or maybe he doesn't realize she's flirting with him."

Jimmy joined them and took a large gulp of beer. "Looks like Ford's getting lucky tonight. He's finally gonna get his cherry popped."

"Hush, Jimmy," Jasmine said with a quick look at Stella.

"What?" Jimmy said. "This is a good thing, isn't it? We want Ford to get laid. Don't we?"

"Yes," Stella said. "If Ford wants to screw some random chick at a bar, that's his choice."

"Meow," Jimmy said with a grin.

Jasmine gave him a dirty look. "Be quiet, Jimmy."

"Sorry, Stella," Jimmy said.

"It's fine," Stella said as Cassie laughed at something Ford said and placed her hand on his arm. "I'm happy for Ford, really."

Liar, her inner voice whispered.

Shut up!

"Stella? It's your turn," Ford said.

She made herself smile at him and Cassie before grabbing her pool cue.

* * *

65

"STELLA, IS THERE SOMETHING WRONG?"

"Why would there be something wrong?" Stella said.

"You seem angry," Ford said.

"I'm not." Stella stared at the pool table as she tapped the end of the cue against the floor.

"Did I do something to upset you?"

She twitched, and the pool cue stuttered to a stop. She sighed. "No, of course not. Listen, I think I'm going to go."

"It's only nine," he said.

"It was a long day at work," Stella said.

"But I thought we were going for coffee after this." He hated how pathetic and needy he sounded, but he only came tonight because of the chance to be alone with Stella later.

You're so pathetic, Ford.

He shoved the voice out of his head as Stella smiled stiffly. "Pretty sure you have other plans now."

"What do you mean?"

She finally looked at him, and he realized how upset she was. He touched her upper arm. "Stella? What's wrong?"

"I told you - there isn't anything wrong," she said. "I'm just being a bitch."

"About what?"

"Never mind. Listen, don't feel obligated to have coffee with me now that you have other plans."

"What plans?" Did he look as bewildered as he sounded?

"Cassie," she said before pointing toward the bar where Cassie and her friends had gone to get another round of drinks. "Your plans with Cassie."

"What?" He blinked at her, and she scowled in annoyance.

"You're going to make me say it? Fine. You're going home with Cassie tonight."

"Why would I do that?" He suddenly felt like he had fallen into the proverbial rabbit hole.

"Why would you... because she's been hitting on you all night," Stella said.

"She isn't hitting..." A flush of red crossed his face.

"She is, Ford. That chick wants to bang you."

His blush deepened. "She doesn't want to bang me. She's just being, uh, friendly."

Stella rolled her eyes. "It's more than being friendly."

"It isn't."

"Oh, please." She stepped closer to him and leaned against him. His dick stirred in his pants at the feel of her soft breasts pressing against his chest. When she trailed her hand down his arm, his nerve endings lit up like they were on fire.

"Oh, Ford, you're so strong." Stella mimicked Cassie's high-pitched giggle. "You must work out all the time. Ford, help me play pool. Ford, do you like my dress?"

She stepped back and rolled her eyes again as he glanced at Cassie. "She's not flirting with me."

"Okay, now you're being deliberately obtuse," Stella said.

"I'm not," he said. "Cassie's pretty and -"

"You think she's pretty?" Stella said.

"Uh, yeah?"

At her look of outrage, he hurriedly said, "I mean, no? It doesn't matter. She's not interested in me."

Stella glared at him before grabbing his arm. "Come with me."

"Where are we going?"

"We're joining Cassie and her friends at the bar. If she doesn't touch you less than five times or rub her skinny, pretty little body all over yours while we're there, I'll concede that she isn't flirting with you."

She marched him toward the three women as he said, "Stella, you're being ridiculous."

"We'll see," she retorted.

They approached the three women, and Ford watched as

Stella reached out to tap Cassie on the shoulder. She stopped as one of Cassie's friends – he couldn't remember her name – said, "You don't get the five hundred bucks without proof, Cass. You have to send us a video of you fucking the freak."

Cassie shook her head. "There's no way I can get a video of us fucking. He'll never agree to that."

"Are you kidding me?" her other friend said. "Of course, he will. Look at him – he'll do anything you ask for a chance at pussy."

Cassie laughed. "You're so fucking crude, Lori. How about if I get a picture of us in bed?"

"Both of you have to be obviously naked," Lori said.

Cassie nodded. "I can do that."

"If you put a bag over his head, you forfeit the bet," the other girl said with a laugh.

"I'll just close my eyes," Cassie said. "At least he's got an amazing body. That'll help make up for the mess he calls a face."

* * *

STELLA GLANCED AT FORD. HIS FACE WAS A DULL RED, AND HIS look of shame and embarrassment sent a lightning bolt of anger through her. Without speaking, he began to back away.

Anger flared brighter within her. Nearly shaking with rage, she turned to Cassie and said, "You stupid mother-fucking dickhead."

Cassie and her friends swung around. Cassie gave her a brief look before smiling at Ford. "Oh, hey, Ford. Ready for another round of pool, handsome?"

"Shut up, you miserable cunt," Stella snarled.

Cassie blinked at her. "What did you just say to me?"

"Stella, let's go." Ford took her arm, but she shook him off.

"You heard me," she said. "You think you're so fucking

hot? Ford wouldn't touch you with a ten-foot pole. You're nothing but trailer trash, you stupid cow."

Cassie flushed bright red and glanced at her friends. "Relax, you fat bitch. It was just a stupid joke."

"Stupid joke?" Stella said. "Are you fucking kidding me?"

Cassie shrugged. "It's not my fault if he's dumb enough to fall for it. Why he thinks any woman would be interested in fucking him with that shitshow of a face is beyond -"

She screamed and stumbled back when Stella lunged for her. She got a fistful of Cassie's shirt before Ford's arm wrapped around her waist, and he pulled her away from the blonde woman. Cassie screamed again as her shirt ripped. Stella, nearly spitting with rage, struggled furiously in Ford's grip.

"Get that crazy bitch away from me!" Cassie shrieked.

Stella swung at her and narrowly missed her face as Jimmy and Jasmine rushed over.

"Let me go, Ford!" Stella shouted as she swung again at Cassie.

With a low grunt, Ford lifted her and carried her toward the front door. Jasmine and Jimmy followed, staring wide-eyed at each other as Stella cursed and shouted. The cold air washed over her heated body, and she glared furiously at Ford when he set her down next to his truck.

"Stella, don't -"

He muttered an obscenity when Stella darted around him and made a break for the pool hall door. He chased her down and carried her back. He set her on her feet again but kept his arm around her waist as she glared at him again.

"Let me go!"

"Not until you calm down."

"I'm perfectly calm," she said. "Let me go."

"I wouldn't," Jimmy said with a wide grin. "She's got murder in her eyes."

Stella scowled at him. Jimmy held up his hands and took a step back. "Hey now, don't give me the death glare, Rocky."

Jasmine giggled, and Jimmy grinned before putting his arm around her. The four of them stared silently at each other until Stella's breathing slowed, and her stiff body relaxed a little.

Ford kept his arm around her waist. She supposed she should have told him he could let her go, but instead, she put her arms around his waist and leaned into his hard warmth. He rubbed her hip tentatively as she stared up at him. Her fury had mostly faded, and she felt sick to her stomach.

"Ford, are you okay?"

"Fine," he said.

"What happened?" Jasmine asked. "Why did you just try to beat up Cassie?"

Ford's face flushed again, and Stella quickly said, "She was talking shit about me."

"What did she say?" Jimmy asked.

"Does it matter?" Stella said. "She was talking shit about me, and she deserved to have her teeth kicked in."

"Huh," Jimmy said. "You know, Stella, you always act so sweet. I had no idea that you were such a badass or that you had a mouth like a goddamn sailor."

Jasmine giggled again as Stella said, "Be quiet, Jimmy."

"Yes, ma'am," he said before giving her a mock look of fright. "Just don't punch me, okay? I'm trying to impress Jazzy, and I'm sure she likes her men with all their teeth."

"I do," Jasmine said so solemnly that Stella couldn't help but laugh.

Ford was still tense. Stella could practically feel it radiating from his body. She rubbed his lower back as Jasmine glanced at her watch. "Well, this has been awesome, but since I'm pretty sure we're banned from the pool hall now, I think I'll call it a night."

Jimmy took her hand. "Allow a gentleman to drive you home, my lady?"

"That's sweet," Jasmine said, "but Ford's having coffee with Stella."

"Ouch!" Jimmy said before slapping her lightly on the ass. "Just for that, I'm only making you come twice tonight instead of your usual three."

"Jimmy!" Jasmine smacked him on the chest before giving Stella and Ford an embarrassed look. "Good night, you guys."

"Night, Jasmine. Night, Jimmy," Stella said.

Jimmy and Jasmine walked away holding hands. When Ford tried to step away from her, she refused to let go of his waist.

"It's late. I should get going," Ford said.

"I thought we were going for coffee," Stella said.

He refused to look at her. "Starbucks will be closed by now."

"We can go somewhere else," Stella said.

He didn't reply, and she said pleadingly, "Please, Ford. I'm not ready to go home."

Ford hesitated. "Are you... I know a good place if you're hungry."

"I'm hungry," she said immediately. It was a complete lie. Her stomach was still in knots.

"Okay."

"Can I go with you? I hate driving in the dark," she said.

Another small white lie, but she wanted to be with Ford.

"What about your car?"

"If you don't mind dropping me off at home, I'll take an Uber in the morning to pick it up."

"Just text me in the morning when you're ready, and I'll drive you over here," he said.

She smiled gratefully at him. "Thank you."

"Sure." He still wouldn't look at her, and her stomach twisted.

"I just need to grab something from my car. I'll be right back."

He had started the truck and was waiting for her by the passenger door when she returned with her camera. He gave the camera a nervous look as he opened the door. "Why do you, uh, have your camera?"

"I always have my camera." She started to step onto the running board, and Ford put his hands around her waist and lifted her into the truck. Her entire body tingled with pleasure at the feel of his hands, and she scolded herself internally as he shut the door.

CHAPTER 7

"So, where are we going?" she said as he drove through the dark streets.

"It's a diner that Henry used to take me to when I was a kid."

"Who's Henry?"

"He's, uh, he works for my family."

"Oh."

They drove the rest of the way in silence. Stella peered out the windshield at the gaudy neon sign blinking on and off above the front door of the building. "Ted's Diner, huh?"

He nodded and parked the truck. Stella slung her camera over her shoulder and was secretly delighted when Ford hurried around to her side. He opened the door, and she didn't object when he lifted her out of the truck and set her on the ground.

"Thank you, Ford." She let her hands linger on his biceps. He stepped back and twitched a little when she grabbed his hand. "Do you mind? The ground is slippery, and I'm wearing heels."

He held her hand firmly, and they walked across the parking lot. She glanced around when they entered the diner. It had a long, curved counter with bar stools, four booths against the far wall, and a few tables scattered around the eating area. Everything was chrome and red leather, and she was immediately smitten with the place.

"I like it. It's very retro."

The diner was empty, and she smiled at the older man who ambled out from the door behind the counter.

"Evening, folks. Have a seat wherever – Ford! It's good to see you again." The man hurried past the swinging door that separated the counter from the eating area and walked toward them. He shook Ford's hand. "Who is this lovely girl?"

"Uh, this is my friend Stella. Stella, this is Ted. He owns the diner."

"It's nice to meet you, Ted," Stella said.

She held out her hand, and Ted shook it before pointing toward a booth. "It's nice to meet you too, Stella. Have a seat, and I'll bring you some menus."

They took off their jackets and slid into the booth.

"He has a jukebox," Stella said in delight. She studied the posters on the wall before grinning at Ford. "I love this place."

He smiled shyly at her. It was the first time he had looked at her since she'd tried to kill Cassie. "I thought you might like it."

"I really do. Do you think Ted would mind if I took some pictures?"

"Don't mind at all," Ted said as he placed menus in front of them. "Take as many as you'd like."

"Thank you," Stella said.

"Can I get you something to drink?"

They both ordered coffee and water. As Ted left to get their drinks, Stella scanned the menu. "What's good here?"

"Everything," Ford said. "I usually get the steak sandwich."

"I think I'll try the chicken fingers," Stella said.

Ted returned and set their coffee and water in front of them. "Made a decision? You want your usual, Ford?"

"Yes, please, Ted," Ford said as he closed his menu.

"What about you, pretty lady?" Ted asked.

"I'll try the chicken fingers, please."

"Fries or salad?"

"Fries, please," Stella said. "I feel like being bad tonight."

"Oh, I doubt a sweet little thing like you knows anything about being bad," Ted said with a grin.

Stella just smiled at him, and he patted her hand before taking their menus and leaving. He disappeared into the kitchen, and Stella took a sip of coffee. "I'm going to take a few pictures. I'll be right back."

She slid out of the booth and snapped pictures of the jukebox and curved counter before returning to Ford. She showed him the photos she had taken. "I think I'll print this one and give it to my mom. She loves jukeboxes."

"Oh yeah?" Ford said.

"Yes. For her birthday last year, me, my dad, and my siblings all went in together and bought her one for the basement. She loves it."

"That's cool."

They sat silently for a few minutes before Stella said, "I'm sorry about tonight."

He shrugged. "It isn't your fault."

She bit at her bottom lip. "It kind of is."

"No, it isn't," he said as he stared into his coffee cup. "Don't worry about it. Besides, it's not the first time this has happened."

Her heart sank into her stomach. "Are you serious?"

He nodded, and she reached across the table and squeezed his hand. "People are awful. I'm sorry."

He pulled his hand away. "I don't need your pity."

"It's not pity," she said so sharply that he glanced at her. "I'm your friend, and something shitty happened to you tonight. What I feel is empathy for my friend, not pity."

"I doubt anything like this has ever happened to you," he said. His voice had no bitterness, but her heart ached for him anyway.

"It has," she said. "Maybe not in the exact same way, but close enough. I'm not exactly the prettiest woman, and guys can be just as cruel as women."

"I think you're pretty," he said, then blushed fiercely. He dropped his gaze to the table, and his blush deepened when Stella squeezed his hand.

"Thank you." She released his hand. "Try not to let assholes like Cassie get to you, okay? The right woman for you is out there."

Maybe sitting across from him.

Hell, yes. At least, she thought so. Unfortunately, Ford might think she was pretty, but he had also been clear that he only wanted to be friends.

He didn't reply, and she searched for something to say as awkwardness descended.

"So, I got some good news yesterday," she said.

"Oh yeah?"

She nodded. "I sent a picture I took of Jasmine to a local photography contest, and I'm a finalist."

"That's great. Congratulations," Ford said.

"Thanks. I'll be automatically entered into a national contest if I win this contest. This local one will give me some exposure as a photographer, but winning the national one will get my photo in a popular photography magazine. It could be the kickstart my career needs."

"Your career?"

"Well, what I hope to be my career. I've started a website and have been doing a bit of local advertising for my studio. I haven't got any actual paying clients yet, but if I win the local and national contest, it could be the boost I'm looking for."

"You'd like to do this for a living, huh?" he said.

"I really would. So, let me know if your friends or family are looking for a photographer. The only thing I don't do is weddings, but I can do headshots, family or couple pics, and baby pics."

"Why don't you do weddings?"

"Honestly? It just feels like too much pressure. The couple is counting on you to provide the perfect pictures for their perfect day. If you take engagement or family pics, you can always try again if they don't work. Not that you want to try again," she said, "but you could if you had to. With a wedding, you only get one shot at it. No pun intended."

He smiled at her as Ted arrived with their food. "Here you go. Eat up while it's hot."

"Thank you, Ted. It looks delicious," Stella said.

"You're welcome, pretty lady."

He left, and they dug into the food. Stella's appetite had returned at the smell of the food, and she dipped a chicken finger into the plum sauce. "Have you given any more thought to posing for me?"

"I'm not photogenic."

"I think you are," she said. "We don't have to do a formal sitting. I could take some more casual pictures. We could try taking a couple right now."

He squirmed a little in the seat. "I don't know."

"Please, Ford," she said. "Let's just try. I can always delete the pictures if you hate them."

He sighed before nodding. "Okay, I guess."

"Thank you!" She smiled with delight before eating some fries.

"Uh, aren't you going to take pictures?"

She laughed. "I'll let you finish eating first."

* * *

"You're really good." Ted glanced at her camera screen.

"Thanks," Stella said. "I've got a good model."

Ford snorted and took another drink of his coffee as Ted cleared their empty dishes. He returned with a pot of coffee and refilled both their mugs.

"Can I take a picture of you, Ted?" Stella said.

He nodded, and she quickly snapped some pictures before showing them to him.

"I've still got it for an old man," he said. "If you don't mind me saying, you might want to adjust your white balance. The fluorescent lighting in here ain't so great for pictures."

"You know photography," Stella said delightedly. She adjusted her white balance as Ted nodded.

"I've taken a picture a time or two. My wife got me a Canon EOS 70D for my birthday last year."

"Nice," Stella said. "What do you take pictures of?"

"Oh, mostly landscapes." Ted sat down beside Ford and put his arm around his shoulders. "Here, take a picture of me and the big lug."

Stella raised the camera as Ted squeezed Ford's shoulder and said, "Try smiling, Ford. It won't break your face, I promise."

Ford grinned at Ted just as Stella took the picture. She stared at the camera screen. "It's perfect!"

She showed it to Ted and Ford. The older man studied

the picture, but Ford only briefly glanced at it before looking away. "It's nice."

"Thanks, Ford."

"Sit beside your girlfriend. I'll take your picture with her." Ted slid out of the booth.

"We're just friends," Ford said quickly.

"Whatever, whatever," Ted said with a wave of his hand. "Sit beside her."

Ford sat down awkwardly next to her. She smiled at him and handed her camera to Ted.

"For Christ's sake, Ford put your arm around her. You look as stiff as a board," Ted said cheerfully.

"Uh, do you mind?" Ford asked.

"Nope," she said.

He put his arm around her shoulders, and she snuggled into him before tilting her head toward his.

"Smile," Ted said.

She smiled and then took the camera from Ted with a nod of thanks. She studied the picture. She was smiling happily, her cheeks flushed looking and her eyes sparkling. Ford wasn't exactly smiling but he at least seemed moderately happy. She showed him the picture.

"You look really nice," he said.

"So do you," she replied. "I'll print a copy for both of us, okay?"

He nodded before glancing at his watch. "It's almost midnight, and Ted usually closes the diner at eleven-thirty."

Ted shrugged. "You two stay and finish your coffee."

Ford slid out of the booth. "That's okay. I should get Stella home. Thanks, Ted. It was good to see you again."

"Good to see you too, my man." Ted clapped Ford on the back before helping Stella into her coat. "You come back with Ford again, will you, Stella?"

"I will. I'll bring you a copy of the picture of you and Ford," Stella said.

Ted kissed her on the cheek. "Thanks, pretty lady. Drive safe now."

They were almost to her house before Ford spoke. "Thanks for tonight, Stella. I had a good time."

"I did, too," Stella said. "Thank you for letting me take pictures of you, and I'm sorry I made a scene at the pool hall."

He shrugged and gave her a half-smile. "I liked seeing the hidden feisty side of Stella."

She laughed as he parked in front of her townhouse. "What can I say? I'm a redhead. It's kind of true about us having short fuses."

Ford shut off the truck, climbed out, and crossed to her side before she could stop him. He opened the door and lifted her out, then took her hand and walked her to her door. "You don't want to slip in those heels, right?"

"Right," she said.

She studied Ford in the dim light of the street lamps. She desperately wanted to invite him inside, but before she could throw caution to the wind and invite him in, he said, "Just text me when you're ready to pick up your car tomorrow, okay?"

"Okay."

"Have a good sleep." He turned and walked away before she could reply. He climbed into his truck and waited until she had opened her door and waved at him before driving away.

Stella closed the door and locked it before leaning against the cool wood. She turned on her camera and stared at the picture of her and Ford, then took off her shoes and slowly climbed the stairs to her bedroom.

* * *

STELLA

Whatcha' doin?

THE TEXT FROM STELLA MADE HIM STUPIDLY HAPPY, AND HE quickly texted back.

FORD

Just watching TV. How about you?

He waited impatiently for her reply. Nearly five minutes later, his phone dinged.

STELLA

Standing outside your front door.

He jerked in surprise before standing and hurrying to the door. It was Saturday night, and it'd been two weeks since the incident at the pool hall. He and Stella had spent almost every night together since then. Most of the time, she dropped by his place after work, and they ate dinner together and watched TV, but last night, they went to Jasmine's house and played cards with her and Jimmy.

This afternoon, she had met him at the theatre for a matinee, but she was quiet and withdrawn. After the movie, she hadn't asked him if he wanted to have dinner together and had left quickly before he could ask her what was wrong.

He opened the door, and Stella grinned at him. "Hey, Ford! What's happenin'?"

"Hi, Stella. What are you doing here?"

"I was in the neighbourhood and thought I'd drop by."

"At eleven at night?" he said.

"Shit." Her eyes widened. "Is it that late? I'm sorry. I'll go."

"No, that's okay," he said.

She leaned forward, weaving slightly, and sighed. Ford could smell whiskey and said, "Are you drunk?"

"Soooo drunk." She giggled. "I couldn't even wear my heels. That's how drunk I am."

She lifted her foot to show him her clunky winter boots. He reached out and grabbed her when she started to tip over.

"Whee!" she said with another giggle before clutching his arms.

"Did you drive here?" Alarm bells were ringing up and down his spine.

"Nope. I Ubered it," she said.

He breathed a sigh of relief as she shivered delicately. He guided her into the house and shut the door, helping her out of her jacket and walking her to the living room.

She collapsed on the couch with a sigh and smiled at him. "Got anything to drink?"

"I think you've probably had enough," he said.

He sat gingerly beside her and tried not to flinch when she squirmed under his arm and leaned her head against his chest. Her red hair was loose and flowing down her back, and he ignored his urge to stroke the soft strands.

"Hey, Ford?"

"Yeah?"

"I'm sorry I was so awful earlier today."

"You weren't awful."

"I kind of was," she said. "I probably should have just cancelled, but I thought seeing you might cheer me up."

"What happened?"

She sighed again. "Remember that contest I told you about? The one where I was a finalist?"

"Yes."

"I got the results this morning by email. I didn't win. In fact, there were five finalists, and I came in dead last."

Her arm tightened around his waist, and he stroked her soft hair this time. "I'm sorry."

"I suck."

"You don't."

"I do," she insisted. "Dead last, remember?"

"You made it to the top five out of thousands of entries. I'd say that's pretty damn good," Ford said.

"I really wanted to win."

"I know you did. I'm sorry."

"Thanks. It's just that I love taking photos, and I really want to make a career out of it. I've taken pictures since I was a teenager and have taken dozens of photography courses. I have a website, I hand out business cards like some crazy person, and I still can't get a single paying client. I feel like maybe I should give up."

"You shouldn't," he said. "You're good at it. Just because it's taking time for other people to figure it out doesn't mean you should stop."

"What if I never succeed?" she whispered. "What if I just keep trying and failing?"

"You won't," he said. "Hell, if you can make my face look halfway presentable in a picture, you can do anything."

She scowled at him. "Don't say stuff like that about yourself. It pisses me off, and you know what happens when I'm pissed off."

He grinned at her, and she poked him in the side. "You might be bigger than me, but I fight dirty. Just remember that."

She pressed her cheek against his chest again. "Do you forgive me for being so awful today?"

"There's nothing to forgive," he said.

"That's nice. You're so nice," she said. "I'm really glad we're friends."

"Me too."

They sat in comfortable silence for a while. His hand still petted her hair, but she didn't seem to mind. She wiggled a little closer and stroked his ribcage. He gritted his teeth and tried to ignore the way his cock was starting to harden.

"God, I'm so drunk," she said. "I probably shouldn't have made my dinner a liquid one."

"Do you want something to eat?"

"No. I'm sorry I came over unannounced."

"I don't mind. You can come over whenever you want."

"At least I texted first and didn't just let myself in with the key you gave me. Although secretly, I was going to, but I couldn't seem to get the key in the keyhole. It took me a good ten minutes to text you."

She laughed. "I'm useless when I'm drunk. Hey, do you have anything to drink? Why don't you get drunk, too?"

"Not a good idea," he said. Jesus, who knows what he would say or do to Stella if he was drunk? At best, he'd confess his pathetic crush on her. At worst, he'd try to kiss her.

"Well, you're no fun." She pouted adorably at him. "I'm tired."

"I can drive you home," he said.

He didn't want to drive her home. Even though she was drunk, he wanted to sit on the couch with her all night. He wanted to touch her soft hair and pretend that she was his.

"No, thank you," she said sweetly. "Hey! I just had a great idea! Let's have a sleepover!"

"I – what?"

"A sleepover! C'mon, it'll be fun."

"I don't have an extra bed," he said. "My spare room is my workout room."

"We don't need an extra bed. We can share yours," Stella said.

His panic must have been obvious on his face because she said, "We've shared a bed before."

"I remember," he said.

She raised her right hand. "I promise I'll keep my hands to myself, and you won't even know I'm there. Also, I solemnly swear I won't look down your underwear this time."

He blushed, and she giggled before slapping her hand against his chest. "Oh God, you're completely adorable when you blush. You know that?"

She relaxed against him again. "C'mon, Ford. I'm way too drunk to be by myself. What if I fall down the stairs at my place and break my neck? You'll feel really bad."

He hesitated, and sensing weakness, she said, "Pretty please? I promise I won't sexually assault you. I know you don't want to have sex with me."

"I don't, that is, it's not that I -"

"Ooh, I just remembered I brought my own drinks!" She slid off the couch and staggered down the hallway. He followed her and watched as she fished a small bottle of whiskey out of her coat pocket. She unscrewed the cap, and he plucked the bottle from her hand before she could drink.

"Hey, that's mine," she said.

"You'll make yourself sick if you keep drinking." He took the cap and screwed it back on. "Come into the living room."

"Sure," she said.

He muttered a low curse when she turned instead of heading to the living room and quickly weaved her way down the hallway to his bedroom. She staggered into the room and flicked on the light.

"Holy moly," she said. "Look at the size of your bed!"

She ran forward and tripped over her feet just as she got to the bed. She fell face-first onto his bed and laughed hysterically before climbing onto it and flipping to her back.

He stood in the doorway, willing himself not to get a full-blown erection at the sight of Stella in his bed.

"Come lie down with me." She patted the bed beside her.

"Stella, I -"

"Please," she said. "I just want to talk, that's all."

He laid down beside her. He groaned inwardly when she flung her arm around his waist and buried her face in his thick neck. His attempt to stop his erection had failed miserably, and he hoped that she was too drunk to notice the obvious bulge in his jeans.

"See how nice this is?" she said. "Sleepovers are fun. Didn't you have them as a kid?"

"No," he said. He had very few friends as a child, and the few he had weren't allowed to stay overnight. His mother always said it was too much work. Of course, that rule hadn't applied to his brother or sister. They were allowed to have friends over whenever they wanted.

"Why not?" Her voice was muffled against his skin, and thankfully, she started sounding sleepy.

"I don't know." He didn't want to tell her that even as a child, he was so ugly most kids didn't want to play with him. Even years later, it was humiliating.

"I had lots of sleepovers." Her soft lips brushed against his throat as she talked, and he made a strangled sound of need. His cock was pressing painfully against his zipper and straining to be free. It didn't care that Stella was drunk. It wanted to be buried in what he was sure was Stella's very warm, very tight pussy.

"Stella, I don't think -"

"I'm so tired." She sat up and yawned before stretching.

His gaze dropped to her breasts, and he fisted the bedcovers in a silent plea for mercy.

"Do you have a shirt I can borrow to sleep in? I left my

pajamas at home. I'm terrible at this sleepover thing," she said.

He nodded. It would be absolute hell having Stella sleep in his bed, but as usual, he couldn't deny her anything. He left the bed and crossed the room to his dresser. With his back to her, he pulled futilely at his crotch and tried to relieve some of the pressure.

He grabbed a shirt and brought it to her as she slid off his bed. "Thanks!"

She staggered into the primary bathroom, and he quickly changed into pajama bottoms. All the spit in his mouth dried up when she opened the bathroom door and struck a pose in his shirt.

"How do I look?"

"Good," he said hoarsely. "You, uh, look really good."

He tried not to stare at her long, pale legs. His shirt was way too big on her and hid the soft swell of her breasts, but he could see a hint of one nipple pressing against the fabric. He turned away quickly to hide his obvious erection.

"Thank you." She tried to curtsy and laughed when she almost fell over. She grabbed the doorframe and steadied herself before walking slowly to the bed. She climbed into the left side, pulled up the covers, and turned her back to him. "Night, Ford."

He shut off the light before climbing in beside her. She didn't make any move to snuggle up to him, and he wasn't sure if it was disappointment or relief he was feeling.

"Good night, Stella."

* * *

STELLA RUBBED AT HER ACHING HEAD AS SHE SAT UP. SHE WAS alone in a giant bed and stared at the unfamiliar room for a minute before the night came flooding back to her. She groaned and fell back on the bed again. God, she had made an idiot of herself with Ford last night. She rubbed at her temples as she tried to remember if she had sexually assaulted him. She didn't think she had. In fact, she was certain that she'd been incredibly careful to stay on her side of the bed and not touch him.

Frankly, that was a goddamn miracle. She was completely hammered last night, and normally, she was super handsy when she was drinking. She squinted at the bedside table. There was a glass of water and a bottle of Advil sitting on it, and she immediately shook out three pills and popped them into her mouth before drinking the entire glass of water.

She sat up and reclined against the headboard while studying Ford's bedroom. It was a nice room, probably a little on the small side, although that might have just been an optical illusion because of the bed. His bed was massive, and she was sure she could stretch out sideways on it, and her feet wouldn't even come close to the edge.

She glanced at the bedside table again and frowned. That made her headache worse, and she muttered a curse before reaching for the framed photo. About a week after the pool hall, she had brought Ford two framed pictures. The first had been the picture of him and Ted. The second was the picture of the two of them. Ford had placed it on the bedside table. But he had folded the photo in the frame, so it only showed her.

Scowling, ignoring how it made her head throb, she quickly opened the back of the frame. She unfolded the picture and smoothed it with her hand before placing it back in the frame. She traced Ford's face through the glass, returned the frame to the table, and slid out of bed. She used the bathroom, brushed her teeth the best she could with her finger, and dressed. She placed Ford's shirt in the hamper and smoothed down her hair. It was time to find Ford and apologize.

He was in the kitchen cooking breakfast, and her stomach made a gurgle of protest at the smell of the eggs.

"Morning," she said.

"Good morning." He smiled tentatively at her. "Are you hungry?"

"Oh God, no," she said. "Could I have some coffee?"

"Sure, help yourself."

"Thank you." She poured herself some coffee and added a healthy dose of milk and sugar before sitting down again. She sipped cautiously at it. "Thank you for the Advil and the water."

"You're welcome. How's your head?"

"Hurts," Stella said. "But honestly, I'm mostly just embarrassed."

"You don't have to be."

She sighed. "I didn't throw myself at you in bed, did I?"

"No, of course not."

"Oh, thank God." If she'd made a move on Ford tonight, she was pretty certain he would end their friendship, which would destroy her. "I'm sorry I just showed up at your house last night."

"It's fine. I'm sorry about the photography contest."

She sipped again at her coffee. "I was disappointed, but it was stupid of me to get drunk and barge into your house."

"You didn't barge in. You texted first," Ford said so earnestly that she giggled.

"Only because I was too drunk to figure out how the key worked," she said. "Do you want your spare key back? I'll understand if you do."

"Of course not. Anytime you want to come over, you're more than welcome. Drunk or sober," he said.

He turned the burner off on the stove. "Are you still planning on quitting photography?"

"No. That was just me feeling sorry for myself. Eventually, I'll get a client."

He sat down, and she reached out and squeezed his hand. "Thank you for being such a good friend. I needed that last night."

"You're welcome." He pulled his hand free and stood up. "How about some toast? You should try to eat something."

"Sure," she said with a soft sigh. God, why did she have to be so pathetic around Ford? He didn't want her touching him, but she kept doing it anyway. "Thanks again, Ford. For everything."

"You're welcome."

CHAPTER 8

"**A**re you and Ford spending Christmas together?" Jasmine carefully added the red carnations to the flower arrangement.

"No, why would we?" Stella leaned against the counter of the flower shop.

"Um, because you've spent nearly every waking moment of the last three months together?" Jasmine tossed her hair out of her face – her long strands were bright green in celebration of the Christmas season – and eyed the flower arrangement critically.

"We haven't," Stella said. "We hang out on the weekends and a few times a week in the evenings."

Jasmine shrugged. "You guys are secretly dating, aren't you? Why don't you admit it?"

"We aren't," Stella said. "We're just friends."

Jasmine peered at her over the flower arrangement. "Sure, you are."

Stella didn't reply, and Jasmine peered at her again. "Stella? What's wrong?"

"Nothing," Stella said.

Jasmine hurried around the counter. "I'm sorry. I didn't mean to upset you."

"You didn't."

Jasmine patted her arm. "I know you like Ford. Why don't you date him?"

"Because he doesn't want to date me," Stella said. "He – he doesn't find me attractive in that way."

"Bullshit," Jasmine said. "I've seen the way he looks at you."

"He doesn't," Stella said. "I don't think he's attracted to chubby girls. It's fine that he isn't attracted to me, but I'm attracted to him, and being just his friend is killing me."

"Why don't you think he's attracted to you?" Jasmine frowned at her.

"Because he never touches me, he never looks anywhere but my face, and he just… he doesn't, okay?" Stella said. "Listen, I'm sorry, but I need to go. Are you almost done?"

"Yes." Jasmine returned to the flower arrangement and added a few more flowers.

"I'm sorry, Jasmine," Stella said. "I didn't mean to snap. I wanted to get to my parents' before six, and it's already five-thirty."

"Why are you still here, anyway? It's Christmas Eve – I thought your office closed at four today."

"It did," Stella said. "Ford and I had coffee and exchanged Christmas gifts. He's going to his family's house for Christmas, and I'm going to mine, so we won't see each other tomorrow."

Jasmine wrapped plastic around the flower arrangement. "I'm going to Jimmy's parents' tomorrow."

Stella grinned at her. "You're not!"

"I am. This is the first time I'm meeting them."

"That's awesome. So, you and Jimmy are getting serious?"

"We are."

"That's great. The two of you need to come over and let me take some pictures of you together."

Jasmine laughed. "Well, you'll need to convince Jimmy. He says he's not photogenic."

Stella frowned. "I'll convince him. I'm in desperate need of some new victims, I mean… models."

"Have you convinced Ford to let you take pictures of him yet?"

"Not in my studio. He lets me take casual pictures of him, but even then, he won't look at the pictures I take. I hate that he thinks he's ugly."

Jasmine didn't say anything, and Stella scowled at her. "He's not ugly, Jasmine. He's unique looking."

"I know that, Stella," Jasmine said, and Stella relaxed a little.

She handed Jasmine her credit card and admired the flower arrangement through the plastic. "It's beautiful. My mom will love it. Thank you."

"You're welcome, honey. Merry Christmas." Jasmine hugged her before giving Stella back her credit card. "I'll see you New Year's Eve, right?"

Stella nodded. "Yes, I'm looking forward to it. I haven't been to a New Year's Eve party in years. Usually, I'm sitting at home alone in my pajamas and binge-watching old episodes of *The X-Files*."

Jasmine laughed. "Well, not this year. Jimmy and I are throwing the best New Year's party ever, and you can't miss it."

"I won't," Stella promised. "Merry Christmas, Jasmine."

She hugged Jasmine once more before walking briskly through the lobby. Ford already left, but Doug was waiting for her. She smiled at him as he walked her to her car.

"Thanks, Doug. I appreciate you walking me to my car," she said as she tucked the flowers into the back seat.

"No problem, Stella," Doug said. "Besides, Ford would have my head on a pole if I didn't. Merry Christmas!"

He waved and jogged back to the building as Stella climbed into the car and headed for her parents' home. She had just pulled into the driveway when her cell buzzed. A smile crossed her face as she read the text from Ford. She quickly typed a reply.

Yes, I just pulled into the driveway. The roads weren't that slippery.

She waited, smiling again when the second text came through.

I'm a very safe driver, Ford Taylor. Stop worrying and have fun with your family. Merry Christmas!

She tucked her cell phone into her pocket and stepped out of the car as the front door opened and her mother waved at her from the doorway. She waved back and, ignoring her urge to text Ford again, headed toward the warmth and light of her childhood home.

* * *

FORD RANG THE DOORBELL AND WAITED PATIENTLY. SNOW FELL lightly, and the entire street was silent. The door opened, revealing an older man with thinning white hair and a lined face. A smile crossed his face.

"Master Taylor, come in."

Ford stepped past Henry and set the bags of presents on the cold tile floor as the butler reached for his jacket. He hung it on the hook, and Ford put his boots neatly next to the others. Faintly, he could hear laughter and Christmas music, and he smiled again at Henry.

"Why are you working today, Henry? It's Christmas, and not even my father would be so cruel as to make you work."

"Technically, I'm not working," Henry said. "Your parents invited me to spend Christmas with them, but old habits die hard, so when the doorbell rang…"

He winked at Ford before suddenly hugging him. Ford returned his hug gingerly, a little afraid of crushing him.

"It is good to see you, Master Taylor."

"It's good to see you too, Henry."

He supposed he should have been jealous of the older man. Henry had worked as his parents' butler for as long as Ford could remember, and his parents treated him better than they had ever treated Ford. But Henry was a good man, one of the best men he knew. Growing up, Ford had wished more than once that Henry was his father.

He might as well have been, he thought. *He knows more about me than my own father ever will.*

Henry patted his face with a vein-laden and trembling hand. "You look good, boy. Happy."

"Do I?" Ford said.

"Yes. What's her name?"

"Who?"

"The girl who's stolen your heart," Henry said.

Ford reddened and rolled his eyes. "You've been watching too many romance movies again, Henry."

Henry laughed. "I do enjoy a good romance." He clapped Ford on the back. "Are you ready?"

"As ready as I'll ever be." He picked up the bags of gifts and followed Henry down the hall to the family room.

Silence fell over the room when he entered. He set the bags next to the Christmas tree and held his hand out to his father. "Merry Christmas, Dad."

His father shook his hand briefly. "Merry Christmas, Ford."

His mother stood just behind his father with a glass of wine in one hand. She turned her face and allowed him to peck her on the cheek. "Merry Christmas, Mom. You're looking good."

"Thank you, Ford." As always, she couldn't quite look at him. She stared at her glass of wine as Ford cleared his throat and took a few steps back.

His brother stood next to the fireplace and downed his glass of whiskey as Ford approached him. "Hello, Dylan."

"Ford."

"Where are the kids?"

"They're with their mother."

"I thought you two had gotten back together," Ford said.

"Who told you that?" Dylan snapped.

"Suzanne. I ran into her at the grocery store and -"

"I said no such thing, Ford Taylor." His sister's shrill voice spoke directly behind him, and he tried not to wince. He pasted a smile on his face and turned around.

"Merry Christmas, Suzanne."

"What are you doing here?" she asked.

"It's Christmas," Ford said. "I wanted to drop off the presents I bought and spend time with my family."

"Well, you can't stay for dinner," she said. Her cheeks were flushed bright red, and she was weaving slightly. "The Fergusons are joining us, and you'll ruin their appetites."

"Suzanne!" Dylan said. "Enough."

"What? I'm only being honest," Suzanne said. "We're used to his face, but the Fergusons aren't. Why should their dinner be ruined just because our brother has nowhere to go at Christmas? Is it our fault that he's alone?"

"Ignore her. She's had too much to drink," Dylan said.

His face a blank mask, Ford turned away from his sister and joined his father again. "How's work going, Dad?"

"Fine. How's the mall security? Busy this time of the year, I would imagine."

"He doesn't work in a mall." Henry joined them, and he smiled at Ford. "You know that, Mr. Taylor."

His father didn't reply. Ford, his stomach churning and his head beginning to ache, smiled at Henry. "It was good to see you again, Henry."

"Are you leaving?" His mother wandered over and sipped at her wine, staring at Ford's chest.

"Yes."

He ignored the relief on her face as his father said, "Goodbye, Ford."

"Bye, Dad."

He nodded at Dylan, ignored Suzanne completely, and left the family room. He grabbed his jacket and shoved his feet into his boots. Before he could escape, Henry was standing beside him, and he patted him on the shoulder.

"I'm sorry, Master Taylor."

"Don't be," Ford said. "It's no different from any other Christmas. When are you ever going to call me Ford?"

Henry grinned at him. "Merry Christmas, Ford."

He hugged Ford again, and Ford clapped him gently on the back. "Merry Christmas, Henry."

He was halfway home when his cell phone rang. His heart fluttered wildly, and he hit the speaker button on the steering wheel. "Hello, Stella."

"Merry Christmas, Ford!" Her voice was a cheerful chirp. "I'm sorry. I know you're with family, but I wanted to say Merry Christmas on the actual day."

"Merry Christmas to you, too. Are you having a good time with your family?"

"Well, I just kicked my brother's ass at crib, so yeah – I'm having a pretty good time."

He laughed as he heard the muted shout of a male voice in the background.

"Shut up, Brandon! You know I wiped the floor with you!" Stella hollered before giggling. "Sorry, Ford."

"That's okay."

There was another babble of conversation in the background, and Stella said, "Yes, yes, I know. Give me two minutes, Mom."

"I can let you go," Ford said.

He didn't want to. The depression that always consumed him after seeing his family had lifted at the sound of Stella's voice. He suddenly desperately wished he could see her sweet face today.

"Hey, are you on speakerphone?" Stella asked.

"Yes, I'm driving."

"Driving? I thought you were at your parents' place," she said.

"I was. I'm heading home now."

"What?" Stella said. "It's only one o'clock. What time do your parents eat Christmas dinner?"

"Oh, uh, I wasn't staying for dinner."

There was silence, and he tried to think of an excuse for when Stella asked why not.

Instead of asking questions, Stella said, "You're coming to my parents' house."

"What?"

"You're coming to my parents' house for dinner. I'll text you the address."

"Stella, no. I can't intrude on your family dinner."

"You're not intruding," she said.

"I am."

"Mom!" Stella shouted. "Can Ford come for dinner?"

"Of course!" He heard the faint voice of her mother.

"We're eating at three, but he's welcome to come over any time."

"See?" Stella said with satisfaction. "Get your ass over here."

"Stella, I…"

"Please," she suddenly said. "I can't stand the thought of you sitting at home alone. I want to see you, okay?"

"Okay," he said.

"Great! See you soon!"

* * *

FORD WAS REACHING FOR THE DOORBELL WHEN THE DOOR flung open, and Stella threw herself at him. He caught her and hugged her as she pressed a kiss against his cheek.

"Merry Christmas, Ford!"

"Merry Christmas, Stella."

"I'm so glad you're here," she said as she took his hand. "Come inside out of the cold."

He followed her into the house and removed his boots as she hung his jacket in the closet. She took his hand again and tugged him down the hall. "C'mon, time to meet my crazy family."

Anxiety churned in his belly. It was always this way when he met new people, and he wished he were normal looking. He wanted to make a good impression on Stella's family, but like everyone else, they would be fascinated and a little repulsed by his looks. He sighed inwardly. He really shouldn't have accepted Stella's invitation. His ugly looks and inability to make small talk would make for a very awkward dinner as Stella's family tried to politely ignore how his face looked.

His steps faltered. He couldn't do this. He couldn't ruin

Stella's family dinner because he was lonely and desperate to be with Stella.

"Stella, I don't think -"

"Stella? Is that your friend Ford?"

A woman stepped out of a doorway and into the hall. Her hair was red, and she looked so much like Stella that she was, without a doubt, her mother.

"Yes! Mom, this is Ford Taylor. Ford, this is my mother, Zoe."

"Nice to meet you, ma'am." Ford held out his hand and grunted in surprise when Zoe hugged him.

"It is so lovely to meet you finally, Ford. Stella has told us so much about you. My goodness, you're a tall one. Aren't you? How tall are you?"

"I'm 6'6", ma'am."

"That must cause havoc when you're clothes shopping." She smiled happily at him before taking his hand and leading him into the kitchen.

"Have a seat. Would you like a drink? We have wine, beer, water, soda, juice. Whatever you'd like."

"A beer would be great. Thank you, ma'am."

"Please, call me Zoe or Mom, whichever you prefer. Most of Stella's friends call me mom," she said.

Ford stared at Stella, who laughed. "You'll get used to her."

"And what exactly does that mean, young lady?" Zoe pinched Stella's cheek affectionately.

"You're amazing?" Stella said.

"Good answer. Grab Ford a beer, would you? They're in the fridge in the garage."

"Sure."

Stella left, and Ford cleared his throat. His gaze dropped to Zoe's feet, and a small grin crossed his face. She was wearing four-inch heels. Clearly, Stella had gotten her love of shoes from her mother.

"Stella tells us that you're an amazing cook, Ford," Zoe said as she stirred a huge pot of potatoes on the stove.

"I like cooking," he replied as a little boy of about three wandered into the kitchen. He stared curiously at Ford, and Ford automatically turned his face away. Children were, at best, intensely mesmerized by his face and, at worst, frightened.

"Nana, I'm thirsty."

"You have a cup of juice in the living room, my sweet," Zoe said.

"I already drank it."

"You did? Well, you can have a glass of water."

"But I want more juice, Nana," the little boy wheedled.

Zoe laughed. "I'm sure you do. You can have juice with dinner. Do you want some water?"

"Okay." The little boy climbed into the chair beside Ford and poked his arm. "What's your name?"

"Ethan, this is Auntie Stella's friend Ford." Zoe placed a glass of water in front of him.

"Hi, Ethan," Ford said. He stared at the table as Ethan leaned closer and tilted his head to stare at Ford's face.

Ford could feel his cheeks turning red as the little boy studied him intently. He waited for Ethan to ask him what was wrong with his face and blinked in surprise when Ethan said, "Do you like to colour?"

"Uh, sure," Ford said.

"Me too." Ethan leaned back in his chair and picked up his glass of water. "I'm really good at it."

Stella returned with his beer, and she twisted off the cap before handing it to him.

"Thanks, Stella," he said as she plopped into the chair across from him.

"Auntie Stella, he likes to colour," Ethan said.

"I'm not surprised," Stella said. "Ford is an artist, Ethan. He's very good at drawing pictures."

"Really?" Ethan said.

Stella nodded, and Ethan slid out of his chair and left the kitchen.

"Mom, what can I do to help?" Stella asked as a dark-haired man entered the kitchen.

"You can start peeling the turnips, please," Zoe said.

"Sure. Ford, this is my brother, Brandon. Brandon, this is Ford."

"Nice to meet you," Brandon said. He glanced at Ford's face before shaking his hand and turning to his mother.

"Dad's asleep in his chair. Should I wake him up?"

Zoe laughed before shaking her head. "No. Ethan had him up at five this morning, and you know your father doesn't do mornings."

"He shouldn't have invited us to stay overnight then." A short-haired woman wandered into the kitchen. She held a baby on her hip and an empty glass in her hand and smiled at Zoe. "Although I won't deny that I enjoyed sleeping in this morning while Ethan bugged Dad."

Stella, peeling turnips at the counter, said, "Ford – my sister, Jocelyn. Jocelyn, this is Ford."

"Hey, Ford. Great to meet you. Stella's told us a lot about you," Jocelyn said. "This is Julie," she stroked the baby's head affectionately, "and I hear you've met Ethan."

"Uh, yes," Ford said. "It's nice to meet you too."

He swallowed a gulp of beer as Jocelyn sat beside him, and Brandon took Stella's spot. Sweat dripped down his back, and he felt odd and unsettled. No one in Stella's family was staring at him. Hell, they weren't even giving him the discreet looks of pity he was used to from strangers. He wasn't sure what to think about that. Maybe Stella had warned them ahead of time about his looks.

Or maybe they're like Stella and don't seem to care or notice what your face looks like.

The thought was a nice one but highly unlikely. No, Stella had warned them not to stare, and they were doing an exceptionally good job of it.

"Boy, you're tall, huh?" Jocelyn said.

"He's 6'6"," Zoe said helpfully.

"Is that why Stella's been wearing her highest heels lately?" Brandon said. "Makes it easier for you two to kiss?"

He made kissing noises as Ford blushed to the roots of his hair. Stella turned and swatted her brother on the back of the head. "Shut up, Brandon! God, you're twenty-four – stop acting like a fourteen-year-old!"

"Are you going to stand there and let her abuse your favourite child?" Brandon asked Zoe as Stella swatted him again.

"Like hell, you're her favourite child," Stella said. "I'm her favourite, and you know it."

"Please, the baby of the family is always the favourite," Brandon said.

"I don't have a favourite child," Zoe said, "but if I did, it would obviously be Jocelyn."

Jocelyn grinned and bounced Julie on her lap as Ethan returned to the kitchen. He was holding a piece of paper and a box of coloured pencils. Ford jerked in surprise when the little boy climbed into his lap.

"Draw a dog," he demanded.

"Ethan," Jocelyn chided gently. "You're being rude."

"He's an artist, Mama," Ethan said.

"I know, but maybe Ford doesn't want to draw right now."

Ethan stared at him. "Will you draw me a dog, please?"

"Sure," Ford said. He selected a pencil and quickly sketched a dog as Ethan watched.

"You're pretty good," he said when Ford finished. "Now, draw an elephant."

He drew the elephant as Brandon leaned forward. "Damn, you're good, Ford. Did you take lessons?"

Ford shook his head, and Brandon gave him an admiring look. "That's impressive."

"Stella, dearest, peel the turnips, please, don't gouge them," Zoe said. "Brandon, can you baste the turkey?"

As Brandon stood and grabbed the baster and a pair of oven mitts, Ethan said, "I have to poop, Mama."

Jocelyn stood and smiled at Ford. "Would you mind holding Julie for a minute?"

"Oh, um, I don't know if…"

"She isn't shy, don't worry." Jocelyn handed the baby to Ford as Ethan slid from his lap.

Ford held the baby and gingerly patted her back as Jocelyn took Ethan's hand and led him out of the kitchen. He had no idea how old she was, and he wondered briefly if he should support her head as she stared silently at him.

Deciding it was better to be safe than sorry, he awkwardly tried to hold her neck, and Stella laughed. "Julie's seven months old, Ford. She can hold up her head."

"Right," he said as more sweat trickled down his back. He hoped the baby wouldn't start crying. It had happened once before with a baby bursting into tears at just the sight of his face. He turned Julie so that she was facing away from him. She immediately turned her little head and stared wide-eyed at him. His discomfort grew as her face twisted. She was going to start crying, and he –

He twitched a little when her face broke out in a wide grin. She squirmed in his arms, and he hesitated before turning her around to face him again. She touched his face with her tiny hand. She pulled at his nose and lips before squeaking happily and resting her head on his chest.

"Aww, she likes you," Stella said. She placed the pot of turnips on the stove and sat beside Ford. She leaned in and kissed the baby's head. Julie grinned at her, and Stella held out her arms.

"Here, Ford, I'll take her. You look extremely uncomfortable."

He handed the baby to Stella and winced when Julie burst into tears. She leaned away from Stella and held her chubby arms toward Ford. Brandon laughed as he closed the oven door.

"Looks like Julie loves Ford more than she loves you, Stella."

Stella made a face at him before handing the baby back to Ford. Julie stopped crying and snuggled against his chest again. He rubbed her tiny back and kissed her head as Stella poked him in the side.

"You didn't tell me you were a baby whisperer."

"You never asked," he said.

She laughed, and he grinned at her.

His head jerked up when Zoe said, "Oh, now that's the sweetest picture."

Stella's mom lowered her phone and showed Brandon the screen. "Isn't that sweet?"

"Sure." He snagged some raw veggies from the platter on the counter before leaving.

"I'm putting this one on the family wall," Zoe said. "Stella, dearest, you'll have to print it for me. You know I can never figure out how to do that from my phone."

"Text it to me," Stella said. "I'll print it and bring it over."

She pulled her phone from her pocket and waited patiently for the picture. Her phone dinged, and she studied the photo before showing it to Ford.

He glanced briefly at it before looking away. He hated seeing pictures of himself and a photo of him sitting next to the gorgeous Stella just reminded him of how ugly he was.

"It's a good picture," Stella said.

"You look great," he said.

"We both look great," she said. "Want me to text it to you?"

He nodded. He avoided looking at pictures of himself, but the urge to have another photo of Stella was too great to ignore.

* * *

"BOY, FORD'S GOT AN AMAZING BODY, HUH?" JOCELYN SAID. She was feeding Julie, and she stroked the baby's soft cheek before shifting her against her breast.

A little tingle of possessiveness went through Stella, and Jocelyn grinned at the look on her face. "Don't worry, Stella. I'm not after your man. After what my dick of an ex-husband put me through, I'm planning on being single forever."

Stella glanced at the doorway of the living room. Faintly, she could hear the men in the kitchen putting away the leftovers from dinner and washing the dishes.

"He's not my man," she said. "We're just friends."

"Then maybe you shouldn't check out his ass every time he turns around," Jocelyn said.

"I don't," Stella protested.

"Oh please," Zoe picked up her knitting from the basket next to her chair, "even I noticed you staring at his ass, dearest. Why aren't you and Ford dating? He's all you talk about and seems like the loveliest boy. A bit quiet, maybe, but lovely."

"Ford isn't into chubby girls," Stella said.

"Did he tell you that?" Jocelyn asked.

"Of course not, but it's pretty obvious. He's mentioned a few times how glad he is that we're *friends,* and he never checks out my awesome boobs. I can take a hint," Stella said.

"That's a shame," Zoe said. "You two are so cute together. But, if you're not going to date Ford, maybe you'll finally let me introduce you to that nice boy, Brian, from church."

"No, thank you," Stella said. "I don't need my mother to set me up on a date."

"I have good taste in men," Zoe said. "You're just being stubborn."

"Nope, just not interested in Brian."

"Because you like Ford," Jocelyn said.

Stella sighed. "Yeah, I do, and it sucks that he doesn't feel the same way."

"Sorry, dearest," Zoe said. "Oh, before I forget – are you joining us for New Year's Eve?"

Stella shook her head. "No, Jasmine and Jimmy are having a party, and I've been invited."

"Ford, too?" Jocelyn asked.

"Yes, why?"

"Maybe you should plant one on him at midnight," Jocelyn said as she tugged down her shirt and placed Julie against her shoulder. She patted Julie's back and grinned at Stella. "I think Ford is more into chubby girls than you realize, honey."

"What do you mean?"

Jocelyn shrugged. "You're not the only one doing some ass checking."

Stella glanced at the doorway again. "Ford checked out my ass?"

"A few times," Jocelyn said. "And you might think he's not noticing your rack, but, honey, you're wrong. He's not perverted about it or anything, but he's noticing the girls."

Before Stella could reply, Ethan walked into the living room, holding Ford's hand. "Come colour with me, Ford."

"Oh, uh, I think I should get going, little man," Ford said.

Stella's stomach dropped, and she gave her mom a *do something* look.

"What? You're leaving?" Zoe said.

"It was nice of you to let me come by for dinner, but Christmas is for family and -"

"Don't be ridiculous," Zoe said. "You're Stella's best friend, and that makes you family. Besides, we'll have pie and our traditional Christmas Aliens movie marathon later. You must stay for it, I insist."

Ford stared at Stella, and she grinned at him. "Dad's got a huge crush on Sigourney Weaver. We watch all four movies every Christmas."

"Well, if you're sure I'm not intruding," Ford said.

"Positive," Zoe said as Stella's father and Brandon joined them.

"Walter, did you remember to start the dishwasher?" Zoe asked.

He grinned at her. "Of course. Ford, come into the study with Brandon and me. I bought a new whiskey, and we'll try it out."

As Ford left the room, Stella smiled happily, and Jocelyn grinned at her. "Make your move on New Year's Eve, Stella, and then call me and tell me all about it."

CHAPTER 9

F ord took the beer from Jimmy with a nod of thanks. He was standing by the window in Jimmy's living room. He glanced anxiously outside for about the tenth time as Jimmy clapped him on the back and walked away.

He was at a New Year's Eve party for the first time ever. He didn't want to be here. He didn't know anyone but Jimmy, Jasmine, and Doug, but Stella was coming, and like always, he couldn't resist the urge to see her. It didn't seem to matter how much time he spent with her. It was never enough.

He'd ignored the stares of Jimmy and Jasmine's friends and planted his large body next to the window, waiting patiently for Stella. He thought they would go to the party together, but Stella hadn't brought it up, so he hadn't either.

He took another drink of beer and glanced out the window again. His stomach twisted painfully when he saw Stella walking down the sidewalk. Her arm was linked with Jimmy's brother's arm. Ford had met him once and thought his name was Greg or maybe Craig. Stella was giving Greg/Craig an amused look as he talked animatedly.

Were they on a date? Was that why she hadn't asked him to drive to the party with her? Disappointment and hurt flooding through him, he turned away from the window and stared into the fireplace.

* * *

"STELLA! HEY, STELLA!"

Stella stopped and stared blankly at the man climbing out of the car. She didn't have a clue who he was, and she tensed when he walked briskly toward her.

"Do I know you?" she asked.

"I'm Greg, Jimmy's brother," he said. "We haven't formally met, but Jimmy's told me a lot about you."

"He has? Why?"

He laughed. "Probably because I've been bugging him for information ever since I saw you at his office building."

She blushed, and he smiled again and shook her hand. "It's nice to meet you, Stella. I love your hair."

"Thank you," she said. "It's nice to meet you too, Greg."

"Shall we?" He held out his arm, and she tucked her hand into the crook of his elbow as they walked up the sidewalk to Jimmy's home.

"So, you should know I'm way cooler than Jimmy," Greg said. "I drive a motorcycle."

She laughed. "Doesn't Jimmy drive a motorcycle?"

"I like to call it his scooter," Greg said. "My bike is way bigger than his."

"Sounds like you might be overcompensating for something," she said, and he burst into laughter.

"Oh, I do like you, Stella. You're just as funny as Jimmy said you were. I have a feeling we'll get along very well."

She gave him an amused look as he smiled at her. "So, ever been on a motorcycle before?"

"No, and I have no immediate plans to do so," she said.

"Hmm, I can change your mind," he said. "By the time summer rolls around, you'll be wearing a leather jacket and have your own helmet."

She laughed. "Are you always this confident?"

"That depends. Do you find it attractive or annoying?"

"At this point, it could go either way."

"I'll tone it down a notch," he said. Stella gave him another amused look as he opened the door and ushered her inside.

He took her jacket and hung it neatly on the coat hook before making a low whistle. "You're gorgeous, Stella. I love your dress."

She smoothed her hand a bit self-consciously down the dark green dress. She had debated about wearing it or not. It was shorter and tighter than she normally wore, and the bodice showed off a rather daring amount of her cleavage. She tugged at the thin straps holding the dress up and took a quick peek to ensure the bustier she was wearing wasn't showing. It was wildly uncomfortable but did a great job of keeping her tits where she wanted them. She didn't fail to notice when Greg's gaze landed briefly on her chest.

He took her hand and tucked it into the crook of his arm again before leading her toward the living room, where they could hear laughter and people talking. When they joined the party, Stella immediately looked for Ford and slipped her hand away from Greg's arm.

Ford hadn't asked her to drive with him to the party, and she'd been a little disappointed. She'd cheered herself up by picturing the look on his face when he saw her in her dress. Not that she had specifically worn the cleavage-bearing outfit for him, but if her sister was right and Ford was secretly into her, he wouldn't be able to resist her in this dress. She was sure of it.

She stroked her hair absently as she swept her gaze across

the room. She smiled happily when she saw Ford standing by the window, but Jasmine grabbed her arm and squealed before she could walk to him.

"Oh my God, Stella, you look amazing!"

"Thanks, Jasmine. You do, too. I love your hair."

"Thank you!" Jasmine touched her bright pink locks. "I decided to go back to pink."

"I love it."

"Hi, Greg," Jasmine said.

"Hello, gorgeous." He pecked her on the cheek before placing his hand on the small of Stella's back.

Stella moved away as Jasmine rolled her eyes. "Go on, Greg. I want to have some girl talk with Stella."

"Sure, but no keeping Stella to yourself all night," he said before leaving.

"Um, Jasmine, is there something you need to tell me?" Stella said.

"Sorry, honey. Greg's kind of obsessed with you. He was visiting Jimmy at work and caught sight of you when you were having lunch with Ford. He's been bugging Jimmy to set the two of you up ever since."

"You're kidding me," Stella said.

"I'm not. What do you think of him?" Jasmine said.

"He's certainly…confident."

Jasmine snorted laughter before drinking wine. "That's one word for it. Listen, maybe give him a chance, okay? I know he comes across kind of strong, but he's a nice guy."

"I'll think about it." Stella's gaze wandered to Ford. Greg had joined him, and she wondered about the look of irritation on Ford's face as Greg smiled at him. "Do Ford and Greg know each other?"

Jasmine shrugged. "Kind of, I think? I think maybe they've met once or twice before. Come into the kitchen with me, and I'll get you a glass of wine."

"I want to say hi to Ford first," Stella said.

Jasmine grinned at her. "He'll be here all night, Stella. Grab some wine, and then you can say hi to Ford."

* * *

"FORD, IS THAT RIGHT?"

Ford looked up, groaning inwardly when Greg stopped in front of him and stuck out his hand. "Yes."

"Good to see you again. I'm Greg, Jimmy's brother. We met at -"

"I remember," Ford grunted.

"Right," Greg said. He watched as Ford glanced at Stella before staring at the floor. "You and Stella are friends, right? I saw you having lunch with her before Christmas."

"Yes."

"Nice. She seems like a sweet girl."

"She is."

"Gorgeous hair and that body – shit, you know what I'm talking about, yeah?"

"You on a date?" Ford said.

Greg nodded. "We are. I've been bugging Jimmy for weeks to set me up with her."

Ford didn't reply, and Greg said, "So, Jimmy said you used to be a Marine. That's impressive. I thought about joining the military when I was younger, but -"

"I have to go. Excuse me." Ford walked away.

* * *

"FORD!" STELLA PUSHED HER WAY THROUGH THE PEOPLE IN THE living room and grabbed Ford's arm. He turned and stared at the floor as she smiled at him.

"Hey, you look really nice tonight," she said as she studied his dark suit.

"Thanks," he mumbled.

She waited for him to say something about her dress. Disappointment shot through her when he continued to stare at the floor.

"What's wrong?" she said.

"Nothing. Just, uh, a lot more people here than I thought."

"It is pretty crowded," she said. "But we can stick together. Safety in numbers, right?"

He just nodded, and she touched his arm. "Ford? Are you angry with me?"

Before he could answer, Greg was standing with them, and she bit back her sigh of annoyance.

"Hello, gorgeous. Miss me?"

"Hi, Greg. Uh, sure. Listen, can you give Ford and me a minute? We're having a private discussion and -"

"It's fine," Ford said. "I need another beer." He walked away before Stella could ask him to stay.

* * *

FORD STARED OUT THE WINDOW OF THE SMALL DEN. IT WAS four minutes to midnight, and he could hear the loud chatter and laughter of the others in the living room. He told himself he slipped away because he didn't want to stand there awkwardly when people began kissing at midnight. It certainly wasn't because he didn't want to see Stella kissing Greg. Nope, it had nothing to do with that. Stella was his friend. If she wanted to date a man who wasn't good enough for her, that was her choice and –

"Ford?"

He whipped around, staring blankly at Stella in that incredible green dress as she shut the door.

"What are you doing in here?" she asked.

"What are you doing in here?"

"Looking for you."

"Why?"

"Why have you been avoiding me all night?" she said.

"I haven't," he said.

"Bullshit."

"Why are you here?" he repeated.

"It's almost midnight. I wanted to celebrate with you."

"You should get back to Greg. He'll want his New Year's kiss." He wondered if she could hear the bitterness in his voice.

"Why would I be kissing Greg at midnight?" she said in puzzlement.

"You're on a date tonight, aren't you?" He winced at the accusing tone.

"Is that why you're being such a dick tonight?" she said. "You think I'm on a date with Greg?"

"I saw you come in together. He was holding your arm and told me you were on a date," he said. "I'm not being a dick."

He turned and stared out the window as Stella snorted softly and joined him.

"We happened to show up at the same time and walked into the party together. I am not on a date with Greg tonight, and I have no idea why he told you we were. I barely know him, and you are *so* being a dick. You've ignored me all night."

She tugged him around to face her, and he shivered when her hands wrapped around his arms. "Look at me, Ford."

"Stella, I…"

There was a loud cheer outside the den as the clock struck midnight. He stared down into Stella's hazel eyes, at the small flecks of green near her pupils as she reached up and slid her cool hand around the back of his neck. She tugged lightly, and like a man in a dream, he leaned down until he could feel her breath on his lips.

"Happy New Year, Ford," she whispered, pressing her mouth against his.

At the feel of her soft lips, he made a harsh, almost desperate groan and slid his arms around her waist. He pulled her up against his body and returned her kiss with a gentleness that seemed to surprise her. His tongue traced her lips, and she opened them eagerly, making a whimper of disappointment when he pulled his head back.

"Ford, please," she whispered.

"Stella," he breathed, and then his mouth was on hers again. He sucked her bottom lip into his mouth, sliding his tongue across it as he sucked gently and then roughly.

* * *

WITH HER HEART POUNDING IN HER CHEST AND HER ENTIRE body quivering, Stella pressed her body against Ford and opened her mouth wide. He slid his tongue into her mouth as one hand curled into her hair and tugged lightly. She let her head drop back as he kissed her repeatedly.

He certainly didn't kiss like a virgin, she thought dimly. In fact, she was certain Ford was the best kisser in the goddamn world. The way he alternated between gentle and firm pressure and the delicate strokes of his tongue was driving her insane. Her entire body was on fire with lust, and she squirmed against him as he captured her mouth again.

Where the hell did he learn to kiss like that?

He bit her bottom lip, and her mind made a startled little yelp before it decided just to shut the hell up and enjoy the experience. This time, his gentleness was gone, and she moaned helplessly when Ford took her mouth in a possessive kiss. His tongue demanded entrance, and she gave him what he wanted as she sagged against him. He held her up easily as their kisses grew more frantic, and she moaned his name.

He lifted her and set her on the desk behind them without speaking. He stepped between her parted legs and pressed his erection against her belly. She moaned again and rubbed against him like a cat. His breath caught in his throat, and she didn't object when he reached behind her and unzipped her dress. He pulled the thin straps of her dress down her arms, and she wiggled out of it as he pushed it around her waist.

He inhaled sharply, his entire body tensing as he stared at her breasts in the bustier. He didn't move a muscle. His hands were frozen into fists at his side as he stared at her. She arched her back in silent encouragement to touch her. He made a harsh groan but didn't move.

"Ford," she whispered, "touch me."

Her whispered plea broke his paralysis, and she moaned happily when one large hand cupped her breast. He stroked her nipple through the satin material, and she made another moan of encouragement.

"So beautiful," he murmured before dipping his head to press a kiss against her collarbone.

She squeezed his waist tightly as he pressed kisses across the delicate skin of her throat. "You smell so good, Stella."

"Thank you," she said. "Do you like my dress?"

"Yes," he said hoarsely.

"I wore it for you," she said.

He sucked on her earlobe, and she made another soft moan as he started to worm his hand under the cup of her bustier and kissed her deeply.

She groaned in frustration when he pulled his hand away. "What's wrong?"

* * *

FORD STARED DOWN AT STELLA. SHE TASTED LIKE WINE, AND alarm bells clanged in his head. Was she drunk again? Was that why she was kissing him?

He moved his hand away, but before he could take a step back, she pulled his hands around her and placed them against the hooks of her bustier.

"Let's take this off," she said.

"Stella," he said anxiously, "are you -"

The door banged open, and Jasmine and Jimmy stumbled into the room.

"Dirty boy," Jasmine giggled when Jimmy squeezed her ass. "You have five minutes to make me come, and then we have to get back to our guests before... Stella?"

Her face bright red, Stella yanked up her dress. Jimmy stared blankly at them before grinning. "Guess we weren't the only ones thinking a quickie at midnight was a good idea."

"Shut up, Jimmy," Ford growled. He turned Stella around roughly. She stumbled in her high heels, and he cursed and caught her around the waist. He shoved her hair out of the way and zipped up her dress.

"Sorry," Jasmine said and yanked on Jimmy's arm. "Jimmy, let's go."

She pulled Jimmy out of the room and slammed the door shut. Stella and Ford stood silently before Stella smiled tentatively at him.

"Ford, I -"

"I'm sorry."

"Don't be sorry. I wanted you to -"

"This was a mistake," he said. He glanced at her before dropping his gaze to the floor and nearly running for the door. "I shouldn't have done that. I'd better go. Bye, Stella."

"Ford, wait! Don't leave," Stella called after him.

He shook his head and jerked open the door.

"Ford!" Stella's voice was angry. He stiffened when she said, "Stop running away! We need to talk."

"I can't," he said hoarsely.

He'd try to kiss her again if he spent one more minute alone with her. Hell, he'd try to fuck her. While she might be drunk enough to enjoy it now, she'd be filled with regret when she sobered up. He cringed at the thought and hurried out of the den, ignoring Stella's angry shout. He grabbed his jacket and left the house, taking deep breaths of the cold air as he ran to his truck.

Chicken! Go back there and explain!

I can't! I'll talk to her later when she's not drunk. If I take advantage of her now, she'll stop being my friend.

You think she's still your friend after you just ran away?

He groaned. His inner voice was right. Stella was furious with him, and she'd probably never speak to him again. Feeling like a coward, he started the truck and drove away.

CHAPTER 10

Ford stared miserably at the sketches of Stella. After a sleepless night, he pulled every one of them from the office and spread them across the kitchen table. Why, he didn't really know. He would never see her again – at least not as her friend – and staring at his drawings of her was pure torture.

The doorbell rang, and he glanced at his naked upper body before trudging down the hallway. The doorbell rang again, and he shouted, "Who is it?"

"Ford, it's me. Let me in."

He froze in place at the sound of Stella's voice.

"Uh, now is not a good time, Stella," he said.

His eyes widened as he heard the key in the lock. Shit! Why the fuck did he give her a spare key? The door opened, and Stella stepped into the hallway. She wore yoga pants, a thick sweatshirt, no makeup, and her hair was in a damp bun. She looked a little tired and a lot angry.

"Stella, this isn't a good time."

She kicked off her boots. "We need to talk. You can't keep

running away every time something sexual happens between us. Listen, I get that you're not into chubby girls, but -"

"What? I'm not -"

"I know you're not," she snapped, "and I'm fine with it. Well, maybe not fine with it, but that's only because I'm tired of wanting someone who doesn't want me."

"You were drunk last night," he said. "What kind of friend would I be if I took advantage of that?"

"I wasn't drunk," she said. "I had two glasses of wine. You think I kissed you because I was drunk?"

She started toward him. "Listen, we need to talk about what happened last night, and I'm not taking no for an answer."

"This isn't a good time. Can we talk later?" He blocked her path to the kitchen when she tried to step past him, and she stared suspiciously at him.

"What are you hiding back there?"

"Nothing," he said. "I'm not hiding anything."

"Do you have another woman here?" Stella's eyes narrowed, and her cheeks flushed bright red. She eyed his naked chest and messy hair as he blinked in confusion at her.

"Another woman? What? Uh, no, that's not it. I just -"

"It's fine, I'll go," Stella said. "We can talk another time."

He sagged against the wall with relief. "Okay, thanks. I'll, um, call later and – son of a bitch!"

Stella darted past him and ran into the kitchen. "If there's another woman in here, I'm kicking your ass, Ford Taylor! Do you hear me? After what happened last night, you had better not…"

He chased after her as her voice died out. He groaned in embarrassment. Stella was staring at the sketches on the table. Feeling sick to his stomach, he cracked his knuckles. "Stella, I'm sorry, I shouldn't have -"

She held up her hand, and he stopped talking as she

picked up a few of the sketches and studied them carefully. "You drew all of these pictures of me?"

"Yes." Sweat beaded on his forehead. If he were lucky, Stella would simply stop speaking to him and not tell everyone what a pervert he was.

"These aren't right," she said.

His stomach dropped, and his hands clenched into tight fists. "I know. I'm sorry. I shouldn't have drawn naked pictures of you. I promise I'll burn all of them and never -"

She turned around. "The breasts aren't right."

"I – what?"

She pointed to the sketch she held in her hand. "My breasts don't look like this, but I guess you've never seen them, so that's not really your fault."

He watched numbly as she sat the sketch on the table before reaching for his sketch pad. A pencil was tucked into the top of the metal coil, and she touched it lightly before flipping through the pages. More half-started portraits of her and only her filled the pages and she glanced at Ford.

"Do you draw anything else?"

"Yes, I usually draw lots of different things. I just, lately…."

She closed the sketchbook with a snap and handed it to him. He clutched it and stared at her in shame. "I'm so sorry."

"Come with me," she said.

He followed her down the hall as confusion and guilt warred within him. He hesitated when she stepped into his bedroom.

She stared at him over her shoulder. "Well, c'mon then."

"Stella, what are you doing?"

She dropped her purse on the bed before pulling her sweatshirt over her head. He swallowed heavily as she stripped off her tank top and reached for the clasps of her plain, white bra.

"You don't have to -"

"Hush, Ford."

All the spit in his mouth dried up when she dropped her bra with the rest of her clothes. He stared at her full breasts, their rose-coloured nipples already hardening in the cool air. Stella stood silently with her arms at her sides as Ford drank in the sight of her naked skin.

He made a harsh groan when she abruptly shoved her yoga pants and panties down her legs and stepped out of them. He stared hungrily at the patch of flame between her legs. She smiled before pulling her hair out of the bun and shaking it out. She climbed onto his bed and reclined against the pillows.

His gaze dropped to the sketch pad in his hand. He was itching to draw her. Now that he knew exactly what she looked like, now that he knew she had small, perfect nipples and a cluster of freckles just above her left breast, he wanted to draw.

He wanted to capture all the details so that when Stella finally realized she was too good for him and stopped being his friend, he could look at his sketches and remember this moment forever.

"Go ahead, Ford."

"What?" he rasped.

"Draw," she said. "I know you want to."

"Are you sure?"

She nodded, and he stumbled to the armchair in the corner of the room and dragged it toward the bed. He sat down and flipped open his sketch pad as Stella smiled again. Her long hair partially covered one breast, but he shook his head before she could sweep it back.

"Leave it," he said.

She smiled a slow seductive smile that made his cock harden. "You're the artist."

* * *

"I WANT TO SEE IT."

It was nearly two hours later, and Ford was closing his sketch pad. He stared hesitantly at Stella as she stretched.

"I want to see it. Sit down on the bed," she said.

He stood and moved to the bed, sitting gingerly on the side as he flipped the sketch pad open to his latest creation. He inhaled sharply when Stella pressed her naked breasts against his back and leaned over his shoulder. His cock went from half-hard to fully erect in an instant. It was embarrassingly noticeable in his track pants, but Stella was staring at the sketch pad.

"You made me look so pretty," she said in soft wonderment.

"You are pretty," he said hoarsely. "You're beautiful, Stella."

"Thank you." She traced the edge of the drawing. "You're incredibly good. You could make a living from this."

"No, I don't think -"

His voice died, and his breath hissed out when Stella slid her hand into his pants and boxers and wrapped her fingers around his throbbing cock. She rubbed gently as she pressed closer to his back. He could feel her nipples poking against his skin, and he couldn't stop his soft moan when she rubbed her thumb over the head of his cock.

"I think so," she said. "I think you could charge people a mint to draw their portraits, and they'd pay it. Have you ever looked into it?"

"Stella, please," he moaned as his hips moved back and forth.

"I'm just saying," she gave a little squeeze to his cock and then nipped his thick neck with her teeth, "you're wasting your talent working security."

Her other hand slid around him and traced the muscles of his abdomen before wandering up and tugging on one flat nipple. He moaned again, and she licked the back of one broad shoulder before sucking on his earlobe.

"Have you imagined this, Ford?" she said. "Have you imagined me naked in your bed and touching you?"

"Yes," he muttered. "Hell, yes."

"What else?" She tugged on his earlobe with her teeth.

"I – what?"

"What else have you imagined? Have you thought about me sucking your cock?"

He jerked against her as his cock twitched wildly in her hand. She laughed. "I'll take that as a yes. What about fucking? Have you thought about fucking me?"

"Every day," he groaned. "Please, Stella."

"I've thought about fucking you too. How good it would feel to have that thick cock of yours in my pussy. It's all I can think about."

"We should stop," he said. "This will ruin our friendship and -"

"Lie back," she said.

"Stella, I can't."

"Yes, you can," she said. "We're friends, right?"

"Yes."

She smiled sweetly at him. "I really need to come. Like, really need it. It would be very *friendly* of you to let me use your cock to make myself come. Don't you agree?"

"We – we can't have sex," he rasped. "Your friendship is too important to me, and I don't want to lose it."

"Of course," she said. "I won't have sex with you. Now, take off your pants and lie back."

He shoved off his clothes and lay on his back. His cock was ridiculously hard, and he blushed a little when Stella stroked him, and precum coated the head. They weren't going to have sex, but maybe after Stella came, she would touch him until he climaxed, too.

He jerked again when Stella straddled his thick thighs. His hands clenched around the sheets as she rubbed his naked chest. "Am I too heavy? Am I hurting you?"

"God, no," he said.

"Good."

He cried out when she wrapped her soft hand around his cock and rubbed back and forth.

"Fuck, that feels so good," he moaned. His hips were rising and falling, and Stella giggled before bracing one hand against his chest.

"It's like riding a bucking horse," she said, giggling again.

"I'm sorry."

"For what?" she said.

"I don't know."

She smiled at him, and every muscle in his body tensed in glorious pleasure when she wiggled forward. She grasped his cock firmly at the base and rubbed the head of it against her pussy. They both moaned as his hands clamped onto her hips. He watched as she pushed the head of his cock past her pussy lips and rubbed her clit with it. She moaned and squirmed with pleasure, her cheeks flushing and her fingernails digging into his chest as she rubbed wildly against him.

When she wiggled back again to straddle his thighs, he stared at her in confusion. "Stella? What's wrong?"

"Nothing," she said. "I want to touch your cock again."

His hips bucked against her, and she smiled a little. "Close your eyes."

He didn't want to. He wanted to stare at Stella forever. He wanted to watch as she touched him and touched herself. He wanted to burn into his mind the memory of how she looked naked and turned on.

"Close them," she repeated.

He closed his eyes obediently and lost himself in the motion of her hand as she stroked him up and down. Dimly he was aware of the sound of foil, but it wasn't until she was rolling the condom onto his dick that he opened his eyes.

"Where did you get that?"

"My purse." She pointed to her purse, which was still sitting at the end of the bed.

"Why do we need it? We're not having sex."

"Yeah, the thing is, Ford," she said as she wiggled forward and rose up on her knees, "I maybe - *kind of* – lied about not having sex with you."

He cried out with pleasure when she pressed the head of his cock against her opening. When she didn't move, he said, "What are you waiting for?"

"Permission," she said. "You said no sex, remember?"

"I've changed my mind," he said.

"Are you sure? Really sure you want to have sex with me?"

"Yes!" he snapped. "For God's sake, Stella – fuck me!"

"Yes, sir," she said with a small grin before sliding his cock into her. She was gloriously tight, and he made a harsh noise of frustration when she stopped.

"Sorry," she panted, "but you're really fucking big. Don't move – I don't want to be split in half accidentally."

She grinned at him, and he stared hungrily at her. "Please, Stella. Oh, please."

"I'm trying, big guy," she said. "Give me a minute to adjust."

He waited, his heart thudding in his chest. Stella pushed and retreated repeatedly until, with a soft gasp, she took his entire cock.

"Oh God," she moaned, "your dick is fucking huge."

"Am I hurting you?" He kept his body completely still, horrified at the idea that he might hurt her.

"No. It feels good."

He moved his hips experimentally, and her back arched as she rode his gentle movement. "Ooh, that's so nice."

He smiled, and she grinned at him before bracing her hands on his chest. "Nice and slow, okay?"

He reached tentatively for her breasts. She arched her back again, and he squeezed gently, then rubbed his thumbs over her nipples. She moaned before leaning over him and resting her hands on either side of his head. Her face was only inches from his, and he automatically turned his head so she wouldn't have to look at his face. She frowned and pressed her hand against his cheek until he faced forward again.

She stroked her fingers against his mouth before pressing her lips against his. He kissed her with an almost desperate need, sliding his tongue into her mouth and licking at her tongue. He used one hand to continue caressing her breast and curved the other hand around her hip. He thrust lightly, and she moaned into his mouth before sucking at his tongue. She nipped his bottom lip and breathed, "It feels so good."

He thrust again, and she pushed back against him before straightening. Her hand moved to her pussy, and he watched as she rubbed delicately at her clit. Her entire body trembled, and he groaned when her inner muscles squeezed his cock.

"I'm not going to last long," she warned breathlessly. Her fingers were speeding up, caressing and rubbing at her clit, and Ford pulled lightly at one nipple.

"Oh, oh God," she moaned.

"I need to move faster," he gasped.

She clutched at one broad shoulder. "Yes, Ford. Yes."

He groaned and pumped his hips rapidly. Her pussy clung wetly to him. He could feel her wetness soaking his thighs, and he curled his other hand around her full hip and held her steady as he thrust back and forth. She was gasping now, her hand working furiously at her clit as she rode him. He was helpless to stop his own climax when she made a soft cry of pleasure and came all over his cock. His back arched, his fingers dug into her flesh, and she held on tightly as his entire body shuddered beneath her, and he made a hoarse cry.

She collapsed against him and rested her cheek against his chest. He stroked her damp back with his fingertips as she traced his biceps.

"Am I too heavy?" she asked.

He shook his head and curved one arm around her waist to hold her in place as his cock softened inside of her. He could stay like this forever – Stella's lush curves felt like heaven – but after a few minutes, she eased off him and curled up against his side. He kept his eyes closed as she petted his chest and kissed his neck.

"Hey, Ford?"

"Yeah?"

"I'm hungry. Will you make me lunch?"

His eyes popped open, and he stared at her as she rested her arms against his chest. She grinned at the look on his face. "What? It's past lunch, and I didn't eat breakfast."

She kissed his chin. "Will you make me something to eat?"

"Yes."

"I want French toast," she said before sitting up. She traced her hand over his abdomen before shaking her head. "God, your body really is amazing."

He watched silently as she stood and headed to the bathroom. She paused in the doorway and raised her eyebrows at him. "Aren't you supposed to be making me French toast?"

He sat up and gave her a small salute. "Yes, ma'am."

* * *

"Is there anything you cook that doesn't turn out delicious?" Stella mumbled around her mouthful of French toast.

She ate another bite, and his cock stiffened when she licked away a drop of syrup from her bottom lip. He wanted her again. God, did he want her.

Don't be greedy. You're an idiot if you think she'll do it again. Maybe she doesn't find you ugly, but you didn't exactly put on a good show earlier. You lasted less than five minutes, and she had to bring herself to her own climax. You could have at least tried to put Diana's lessons to good use, asshole.

He looked away as Stella sucked the syrup from the tip of one finger. He had barely touched his French toast, but she had eaten with gusto. He was still too goddamn horny to have much of an appetite. He closed his eyes. Sex with Stella was amazing, but knowing that this would be his only taste of her, and he would spend the rest of his life craving more, sent a wave of depression crashing through him.

"Ford? What's wrong?"

"Nothing." He opened his eyes and smiled at her. "Do you want more food?"

"Nope, I'm full. Thank you."

"You're welcome."

He waited for her to say she had to leave. Diana had left immediately after sex, her desire to get away from him more than obvious. Although he knew Stella wasn't like Diana, he could see no reason why she would stay. Hell, she was probably already regretting what she had done.

She pushed her plate away and typed something into his iPad. She had asked to borrow it, and he watched as she bit her lip in concentration before typing again. God, she was so fucking sexy. She had joined him in the kitchen wearing one of his t-shirts, and he'd felt an odd little trickle of pleasure. This was his second shirt that would smell like her now, and he would tuck it away with the first one and never wash either of them again.

"Here, look at this." She passed the iPad to him, and he stared in confusion at the screen.

"Why are you showing me this?" he asked.

"Because I only had one condom in my purse." She popped the last of her French toast into her mouth.

He stared at her medical records, barely registering them as she laughed and said, "If I had known the day was going to end up like this, I would have shoved the entire box in my purse."

"I don't understand. Why do I need to see your medical records?"

She stared at him in puzzlement. "So you can see that I was recently tested and am negative."

"But we used a condom," he said stupidly.

"Yes," she said. "But I don't have any more in my purse, and I didn't see any condoms in your medicine cabinet. I could go out and buy some more, but I figured it would be easier if we just showed each other our medical records. I'm on the pill, by the way, so you don't have to worry about being my baby daddy."

She laughed and wiggled her eyebrows at him as he said, "You want to have sex again?"

"Yes. Don't you?"

He didn't reply, and her face fell. "Oh shit. You don't."

She slapped herself on the forehead. "Stella, you idiot! Christ, this is embarrassing."

She jumped up and carried her plate to the sink. "I'm sorry. I just assumed you had as much fun as I did and…"

She called herself an idiot again before smiling weakly at him and heading toward the doorway. "So, I'm gonna go because I am absolutely mortified and I -"

"I want to have sex with you!" he shouted.

She jumped, and he blushed. "I'm sorry. That was loud."

"Are you sure?" she said. "I'm starting to feel like maybe I coerced you into having sex with me earlier. I'll understand if you don't want to, and I won't go all crazy if you only want to be friends. I don't want you to feel forced into doing something you don't want to do."

"I don't," he said with an embarrassing tinge of desperation. "I want to have sex with you again, Stella."

His fingers trembling, he logged out of Stella's medical records and quickly logged into his own before shoving the iPad across the table. "These are mine."

She scanned his records, and still blushing, he said, "I know the tests were from a while ago, but I haven't been with anyone since then."

She set the iPad on the table, and he groaned when she straddled his lap. A small smile crossed her face before she rubbed against his erection. "Well, I was going to ask if you were certain about letting me sex you up again, but I think I have my answer."

"I want you so much," he whispered.

"I want you too," she said before sucking lightly on his neck.

She gasped when he gripped her ass and stood up. She wrapped her legs around his waist and clung to his shoulders. "Ford! One of these days, you'll hurt your back carrying me around."

"Not likely," he said as he walked to the bedroom. "You're not heavy."

She laughed. "Well, I'll let you get away with that fib because I've never been carried to a bedroom before, and I'm really enjoying it."

He set her down on the bed, and she squeezed him with her legs before releasing him. He reached for the hem of her shirt, and she helped him pull it over her head. She was naked underneath it, and he stared hungrily at her.

"Lie back," he said hoarsely.

She laid back obediently, and he took off his track pants and stretched out beside her, resting one big hand on her tummy. He leaned over her and kissed her upper chest before licking between her breasts. She moaned and grabbed his head, holding his hair tightly in her fists as he licked the underside of each breast before nipping and kissing the sides of them. Her nipples were erect little buds, and he traced circles around them with his tongue as she moaned and moved restlessly beneath him.

He pushed his thigh between hers, and she immediately thrust her pussy against his leg, rubbing herself almost frantically against his rough skin. He continued to tease her, licking and kissing around her swollen nipples but refusing to suck on them until she huffed in frustration and whacked him on the back.

"Stop teasing!"

He grinned, and Stella cried out when his wet mouth closed around her right nipple. He sucked gently then firmly, varying the pressure of his mouth as his fingers played with her left nipple. She arched her back and made the most delightful cooing noises of pleasure as he tugged on her nipple with his teeth.

He stopped abruptly, and she pouted at him. "Please."

Without replying, he lifted her arm and kissed the inside of her elbow. She shivered all over and gave him a wide-eyed, pleading look as he licked down her arm and nuzzled her wrist.

"Ford," she whispered, "you're driving me crazy."

Stella moaned when Ford lifted her hand to his mouth and sucked on her index finger. She rocked her pussy against him frantically.

"I can't take anymore," she whimpered when he kissed across her stomach and picked up her left hand.

"Really? Because I'm just starting," he said teasingly.

"Oh my God," she moaned and closed her eyes as he sucked gently on each finger.

Twenty minutes later, with her breath coming in short, harsh pants, Stella stared pleadingly at him. "If you don't fuck me, I'll go insane."

Ford licked her calf again and smiled at her. "I'm almost done."

"Almost done?" she moaned. "You've licked and kissed every part of my damn body. I can't – I mean, I really can't - take the teasing anymore. Please!"

"Not every part," he said as he kissed her kneecap. He pushed her thighs open, and he heard Stella's breath catch in her throat when he licked the inside of her thigh.

He kissed his way up her leg, and when she felt his warm breath on her pussy, she arched her back. He touched the line of freckles just above her pubic hair with the tip of his tongue.

"I love your freckles, Stella."

"Thank you," she muttered before winding her fingers in his hair and trying to push his head downward.

He laughed and kissed each freckle before nuzzling her pubic hair. She moaned and wiggled wildly beneath him. "Oh God, please, Ford."

He stared at her wet core. Liquid gleamed on her lips, and he could see her swollen clit peeking out from between them. He licked away the moisture, and she made a breath-less scream of pleasure as her entire body arched. Smiling, he slid his tongue between her lips and licked her clit lightly before sucking it into his mouth. Her body convulsed under him as she climaxed immediately. He licked her clean as she shuddered and moaned and pulled at his hair. When her body relaxed, he kissed her pussy and moved up her body, positioning himself between her splayed thighs.

"Holy mother of God," she whispered as he kissed each breast tenderly before reaching between their bodies. He guided his cock into her and pushed experimentally. He slid in easily into her wet heat, and he groaned under his breath as her pussy clenched around him with the last of her orgasm.

Stella touched his face as he moved in and out of her in a gentle motion. He held her gaze for a moment, then bent his head and buried his face in her neck. She threaded her fingers in his hair and tugged until he was looking at her.

She cupped his face and kissed his mouth. "Don't look away from me."

He stared at her as he thrust slowly back and forth. She gripped his ass and lifted her hips to meet each of his slow thrusts, moaning quietly every time he pushed into her.

"Am I hurting you?" he asked worriedly.

Stella was tighter than Diana, and even though it felt amazing, he would stop if it hurt her.

"No," she said. "It feels really good. Move faster."

He did what she asked, turning his face to the side out of habit as he pushed forward. Her soft hands cupped his face and turned him back toward her.

"Keep looking at me," she whispered. "I want to watch your face as you come."

Her low words turned him on almost as much as the smooth grip of her pussy. He groaned and fucked her roughly. She gasped with pleasure and clutched his broad shoulders as he drove in and out of her with rough, hard strokes.

"Stella," he moaned, "you feel so good."

She smiled and hooked her legs around his hips before squeezing him with her inner muscles. He made a hoarse moan, and she squeezed him again as she dug her heels into his back.

"Harder," she said.

He did what she asked, bouncing her into the mattress as she moaned and arched her back.

"Oh, oh, oh," she chanted. Ford made another hoarse groan when her entire body shuddered around him, and she came all over his cock. Her pussy squeezed him rhythmically as her orgasm coursed through her, and he cried her name before climaxing deep inside of her.

She cupped his face, watching him intently as he shook, and then moaned her name again. She kissed him, and he whispered, "You're so beautiful."

She smiled prettily and kissed him again. "So are you."

He eased out of her and rolled to the side. She cuddled into him, slinging her arm around his waist and resting her head on his chest. He held her tightly. He was afraid she would get up and walk out, but she didn't move.

She's not going to leave. She's not Diana.

No, she wasn't, but he didn't want to set himself up for disappointment if she didn't stay.

"Ford?" she said.

"Hmm?" He stroked her back.

"You're really good at sex."

He laughed, and she rested her arms on his chest before smiling at him. "I mean it."

"Thank you. You're amazing, too."

"Thanks," she said. "You should know that I'm going to ask you to eat my pussy a lot. Your tongue is like magic."

He blushed furiously, and she laughed again and kissed his chest. "Sorry, I didn't mean to embarrass you."

She rested her head on his chest again. "Will you spend the day with me?"

"Yes," he said. "I'd really like that."

"I would, too."

He glanced at the alarm clock. It was just after three in the afternoon, and he squeezed her hip lightly. "Did you want to go to a movie or something?"

She shook her head. "No, I don't want to go out."

"That's fine. We could find something on Netflix and -"

"Ford?"

"Yeah?"

"Don't take this the wrong way because you know I love watching movies with you, but when I asked you to spend the day with me, I meant I wanted you to fuck my brains out."

Happiness flooded through him. Stella sat up again and smiled at him. "I'll assume by the look on your face that you're cool with that?"

He nodded quickly. "Yes."

"Good."

CHAPTER 11

Ford stroked Stella's long hair as she shifted into a more comfortable position on the couch. He couldn't seem to stop touching her, but she didn't seem to mind. She leaned against him, her hair brushing against his naked chest and her hand stroking his thigh. He ran his fingers over her arm, marveling at the softness of her skin. He wanted to bury his face in her neck and inhale her scent but made himself turn back to the TV instead. He pulled her a little closer, and she squeezed his thigh.

It was almost ten, and they'd been napping and having sex for most of the day. He made her dinner, and they had another round of sex before she suggested watching some TV. She would leave soon, and maybe he wouldn't see her again until Monday. His stomach churned, and the thought of two Stella-less days loomed over him like a dark thundercloud.

His arm tightened around her, and she glanced at him before rubbing his thigh again. He shifted a little. His dick was starting to harden, and he cursed to himself. It had been years since he'd had sex, and he was embarrassed at his lack of self-control. He tried to move away from the touch of her soft hand, and Stella frowned at him.

"What's wrong?"

"Uh, nothing," he said.

She glanced down, and a small smile crossed her face. He inhaled sharply when she moved her hand to his crotch and rubbed.

"You're insatiable," she teased.

"I'm sorry," Ford said.

"Don't be. I like it. Although," she hesitated, and his heart made a quick drop to his ankles, "I'm a little sore, so I think if I want to be able to walk tomorrow, we'd better not have sex again tonight."

He stared anxiously at her. "I'm so sorry, Stella. I didn't mean to hurt you."

"It's not your fault," she said. "Don't worry about it. It's been a while for me, and you're much bigger than I'm used to."

She was still rubbing his cock, and he stared at her in confusion when she said, "But that doesn't mean I can't make you feel good."

"What do you mean?"

She blinked at him before giggling. "Oh my God, you are so damn sweet."

She slid off the couch with a small wince. Ford's eyes widened when she pushed his thighs apart and knelt between his legs.

"Oh God," he said when she stripped off his shirt and dropped it on the floor. She was naked under it, and he stared at her breasts as she gave him a wide smile.

"Hips up," she said as she curled her fingers around the waistband of his pants. His heart beating frantically in his chest, he lifted his hips, and she dragged down his pants. She pulled them off his feet and tossed them aside before wrapping her hand around the base of his cock and squeezing firmly.

He groaned as she stroked him roughly, then pressed a soft kiss on his knee. She kissed her way up his thigh before leaning forward and kissing just above his navel. Her breasts were rubbing against his cock, and he jerked compulsively as precum smeared across her breasts.

"I'm sorry," he whispered.

"It's fine," she said as more precum leaked out of his cock. "Let me clean that up for you."

Every nerve ending in his body lit up, and his entire body tensed in anticipation as she lowered her mouth toward him. He closed his eyes. An image of Diana and the look of disgust on her face when he'd asked her to go down on him immediately coursed through him. He pushed lightly on Stella's shoulders.

"What's wrong?" she asked.

"Stella," he said hoarsely, "you know you don't have to do this, right?"

"Yes," she said. "I want to."

"Are you – are you sure?"

Fuck, man! Have you gone crazy? Shut up and let her suck your dick!

"Very." She licked her lips before smiling seductively. "Don't you want my mouth?"

"Yes," he rasped. "You have no idea how much I want that."

"Then be quiet and let me suck your cock," she said primly.

His laugh turned into a loud moan at the feel of her hot, wet mouth. His hips bucked forward, and she made a muffled sound of surprise before lifting her head and grinning at him. "You like that, huh?"

"Stella," he begged, "please. Oh, please."

He could hear the absolute desperation in his voice, but he was beyond caring. He wanted Stella's mouth again and, at that moment, would have done and said anything to her to get it. A frown line appeared between her eyes, and she gave him an odd look.

"Please," he moaned.

She dipped her head and slid her mouth down over his cock. She sucked hard, and he made a hoarse cry as his hips thrust up again. She gripped the base of his cock and sucked before teasing the head of his cock with her warm, wet tongue.

He cried her name and buried his hands in her long red hair. He gripped it tightly as she dragged her mouth up and down his cock. She twisted her hand lightly around the base, squeezing and stroking as she sucked on just the head.

Ford could barely breathe. Her mouth was as warm and smooth as her pussy but different - so fucking different - and he was already close to coming. He tried to hold back, tried to stop the orgasm that was building at the base of his cock. But when she took more of his cock into her mouth and sucked firmly, he lost control.

She made another muffled noise of surprise when his body jerked, and he climaxed in her mouth. She swallowed his warm seed and kept her mouth wrapped around him as he came. He twitched and moaned as she pumped him with her hand until he was completely spent.

She sat back on her heels, licking her bottom lip as he collapsed against the couch and stared wide-eyed at her. She didn't say anything, and after a moment, he said, "I'm so sorry."

Naked, she climbed into his lap and rested her head on his shoulder. "For what?"

"I should have warned you, should have told you that I was..."

She rubbed his chest with her warm hand. "That was hands down the best reaction I've ever gotten when giving a man a blow job. Trust me, I didn't mind."

He stroked her smooth thigh, but she sat up before he could slip his hand between her thighs.

"Ford, can I ask you a question?"

"Yes."

"Was that your first blowjob?"

He dropped his gaze to her lap, and she rested her forehead against his. "Was it?" she asked in a gentle tone.

"Yes."

He could feel shame creeping in, but Stella straightened and stared at him in astonishment. "Good Lord, you should have told me you've never had a blowjob. I would have given you one much earlier."

He blushed, and she grinned at him before kissing the tip of his nose. "I'm glad I was the first woman to give you a blowjob."

"I'm glad too, Stella. It was amazing."

She kissed him before snuggling against his chest again. They sat in silence for a few minutes as he rubbed her back.

"It's getting pretty late," she said.

He pulled her a little closer. He didn't want Stella to leave, but he didn't want to push her to stay the night if she didn't want to. "Yeah."

"It's cold and dark," she said. "Have I ever told you that I have terrible night vision?"

He hesitated and said, "You could stay the night with me."

She sat up and grinned happily at him. "I would love to. If you don't mind?"

"No, I'd like you to stay the night."

"Good. Let's go to bed."

"What side do you sleep on?" she asked when they were in the bedroom.

He shrugged. "It doesn't matter."

She stared at him in horror. "Doesn't matter? I can't believe I had sex with a guy who doesn't have a firm 'I sleep on this side of the bed' stance."

He laughed as she dropped his hand and climbed into the left side. "Of course, it does make it easier for me to claim the left side."

He slid into the bed beside her as her look turned serious. "This is my side from now on. Got it?"

"Yes," he said with a small grin.

She laid down on her back, and he put his arm around her waist and buried his face in her neck.

"Your bed is really long," she said. "I suppose it would have to be. Did you have it custom made?"

"Yes." He cupped her breast, teasing her nipple with his fingers and smiling when she made a soft moan.

"Ford," she placed her hand over his, "there is nothing I would love more than to fuck you right now, but I probably should give my girlie bits a break."

"I know," he said as he trailed his hand down her abdomen and cupped her pussy. "But that doesn't mean I can't make you feel good."

He rubbed her clit, and she moaned before wrapping her hand around his thick wrist. "You make an excellent point, Ford Taylor."

He nuzzled her neck. "Does that mean you want me to keep going?"

"Yes," she said breathlessly. "Make me feel good, big guy."

"Yes, ma'am."

* * *

"HOLY SHIT! I HAVE TO GO – RIGHT NOW!"

Ford sat up in bed, staring blearily at Stella. She climbed

out of bed and stumbled around the room, searching for her clothes. She dressed hurriedly and tried to smooth her hair down.

"Stella? What's wrong? Did I do something wrong?"

"What? No, of course not," she said. "But I'm supposed to be at my sister's for lunch in," she glanced at his alarm clock, "shit! Twenty-three minutes."

She suddenly made a face. "Do you have a toothbrush I can borrow?"

"Yes. There are extras in the medicine cabinet."

"Perfect!" She darted into the bathroom, and he rubbed his hand across his face. Stella woke him at five this morning and gave him another blowjob. Like before, he lasted less than three minutes with her hot mouth teasing him, and another trickle of embarrassment went through him. She hadn't seemed to mind, though. She even commented about his quick recovery time when he went down on her and then made love to her again. Worried she was too sore, he tried to be gentle and slow. But by the end, she was pounding him on the back and begging him to move faster.

Stella reappeared in the bedroom, grabbing her purse before hurrying to the bed. She kissed him and squeezed his arm. "I really have to go. I'll text you later, okay?"

"Uh, okay. Bye, Stella."

"Bye!"

* * *

"WHAT IS GOING ON WITH YOUR HAIR?" JOCELYN SAID AS Stella hurried into the house.

"Nothing. What do you mean?" Stella smoothed her hair down.

"Have you just given up on brushing it now?" Jocelyn said.

145

"Shut up. It's a bad hair day, okay?" She brushed past Jocelyn and went into the kitchen. "Where are the kids?"

"Ethan's at a friend's house, and Julie is napping." Jocelyn leaned down and sniffed at Stella.

"What are you doing? Stop sniffing me, you weirdo," Stella said.

"Why do you smell like Ford?"

"Why do you know what Ford smells like?"

"He wears nice aftershave. I noticed it at Christmas." Jocelyn grabbed two bowls and spooned some soup into them.

Stella inhaled deeply. "Oh God, that smells so good. Thanks, Jocelyn, I'm starving."

"I'm sure you are," Jocelyn said. "Sex burns a lot of calories."

"It really does," Stella said.

"So, my advice about planting one on him on New Year's Eve worked," Jocelyn said smugly. "This is why you should always listen to your big sister."

"Actually," Stella said, "I did kiss him on New Year's Eve, but he kind of freaked out when we were interrupted by Jasmine and Jimmy and then ran away. But I went over to his place yesterday, and we," she paused, "worked things out."

"Well, that explains the hair," Jocelyn said.

Stella laughed. "I stayed the night at Ford's and slept in. You're lucky I'm fully dressed and brushed my teeth."

"Was Ford a virgin?" Jocelyn asked.

"Jocelyn!" Stella glared at her. "Why would you think that?"

"Because Ford has unconventional looks, and we women can be shallow bitches," Jocelyn said.

Stella sighed. "Yeah, we can be. But no, he wasn't a virgin. In fact, he was good. Really good. Like, he does this rolling thing with his hips that…"

Jocelyn grinned at her. "Don't spare me the dirty details. I want to know everything."

"It was the best sex of my life," Stella said. "His body is unbelievable, and he's so damn strong. I don't have to worry about squishing him with my chub. He's an amazing kisser, and he takes his time with everything. Every time, and I mean *every* time, he went down on me, he spent like half an hour kissing my entire body first. He always gave me at least two orgasms before he let himself have one. Truthfully, before we had sex, I thought he probably was a virgin, but he definitely wasn't. Hell, I'm starting to think he's had more partners than I have."

"Good for you, honey," Jocelyn said before eating more soup.

"Very good for me," Stella agreed. "He does have some… weird idiosyncrasies, though."

"Like what?"

"Well, every time we're having sex, he looks away from me. If I'm not physically holding his face, he either turns it away or buries it in my shoulder."

Jocelyn shrugged. "Some guys don't like to be looking at their partner when they're having sex. It can be too intense for them."

"Yeah, I guess, but it doesn't feel like that's what it is. It's almost like he's been, I don't know, taught to look away," Stella said. "Also, I'm pretty certain he's big into cuddling and touching when we're not in bed, but he holds back. He'll start to touch me and then snatch his hand away like he thinks I'm going to yell at him. It's so weird. And as good as he is in bed, he'd never had a blowjob before."

"Really?"

"Really. You should have seen the look on his face when I went down on him. He was like a kid in a candy store."

She ate a few more bites of soup. "I don't understand why

he's never had one, Jocelyn. Obviously, he's got skills, and I'm assuming one of his past girlfriends gave him a lot of tips on how to please a woman, but why wouldn't she or any of the others have gone down on him?"

"Some women aren't into blowjobs," Jocelyn said.

"Well, that just seems selfish."

Jocelyn laughed. "So, are you and Ford dating now or what?"

"I don't actually know. I had to leave quickly, and we didn't do much talking over the past twenty-four hours. I said I would text him later."

"Do you want to date him?"

"You know I do," Stella replied. "I think he wants to date me too, but he's so damn shy and an introvert. I'm like the exact opposite of that."

"Opposites attract," Jocelyn said. "Besides, you guys are already best friends, so obviously, it works for you."

"Yes, but I don't want to scare him off. Sometimes, I come on a little strong in new relationships. I get the feeling that he's been alone for a long time and that it doesn't bother him all that much. If I get into his personal space too much, it's bound to annoy him. I'll take things slow and not push him too hard for a relationship. I'll text him later and keep things casual. If he asks me to come over, that'll be great, but I won't just invite myself to his place."

"I don't know," Jocelyn said, "Ford seems to be really into you, Stella."

Jocelyn stood at the faint sound of Julie crying. "Be right back. The princess is awake."

Stella stared at her half-empty bowl of soup. She really needed to take things slow with Ford, so why was she anxious to get back to him? The temptation to go home, shower, and return to Ford's house was ridiculously hard to deny.

No, Stella. Take it slow, you idiot. Do you want to lose Ford?

No, she definitely didn't. She would play it cool and not act like she wanted to spend every waking moment with him.

* * *

"WAY TO PLAY IT COOL, MORON," STELLA MUTTERED. Balancing the two coffees carefully, she rang Ford's doorbell.

She had texted him yesterday afternoon, just a quick hello and apology for running out on him. He immediately returned her text and told her not to worry about it. She had waited with her heart in her throat for him to suggest they get together, but he hadn't texted again.

She spent a boring evening at home, checking her phone every five minutes and flipping aimlessly through the channels before finally going to bed at nine. She was tired but tossed and turned for most of the night. Finally, she got up at six, showered, and then drove to Starbucks and picked up coffee for her and Ford.

She took a deep breath. She was just being friendly. Ford loved coffee, and unlike her, he was an early riser. She would drop off the coffee, make some small talk, and then leave.

The door opened, and the smile froze on her face as lust made a sudden and very unexpected appearance. Ford was wearing just a pair of gym shorts, and he stared at her in surprise.

"Stella? What are you doing here?"

She swallowed her urge to toss the coffee and climb him like a tree. "Hi, Ford. I, uh, brought you coffee."

She held the coffee out to him like a peace offering and tried to avoid looking at his naked chest. He was covered in a light sheen of sweat, and the muscles in his arms looked somehow bigger.

"What are you doing up so early?" he asked.

"I couldn't sleep, and I knew you'd be awake, so I figured I'd bring you some coffee."

He continued staring at her, and feeling like a loser, she shoved the coffee into his hand and turned to leave. "I'm sorry, I shouldn't have just shown up like this."

"No, Stella, wait!"

She turned back as her stomach churned with anxiety and lust. Ford cleared his throat. "Come in. I was working out."

Well, that explained the bulging muscles.

She followed him into his house. "I don't have to stay. I didn't mean to interrupt."

"No, it's fine. I can finish later."

"Oh no, go ahead and finish," she said. "I can wait."

God, why did things feel so awkward between them?

"Are you sure?" he said.

She took a sip of her coffee. "Absolutely. No problem."

"Uh, okay. I'll be another ten minutes or so."

He set the coffee on the kitchen table and disappeared down the hallway. She bit her bottom lip and paced quietly for a few minutes. She removed her jacket and draped it across the chair before pulling self-consciously at her t-shirt. She told herself that she hadn't worn a low-cut t-shirt or tight jeans for any particular reason. She certainly hadn't worn her red push-up bra with the matching red panties because she thought Ford might be seeing them. No, she just wanted to feel pretty today.

Fifteen minutes passed, and her stomach dropped when Ford didn't reappear. She was making a fool of herself. She thought about sneaking out and scolded herself fiercely for being so immature. She would pop her head into Ford's exercise room and say a quick goodbye. It had been a mistake to come over. She was fucking this up already, and she was determined to fix it before it was too late.

She could play it cool. She could wait for Ford to decide he wanted to see her again.

No problem.

* * *

GRUNTING LOUDLY, FORD HEAVED THE BAR OF WEIGHTS upward. He had been doing chest presses for the last fifteen minutes, and his entire upper body was starting to shake. He needed to stop. He had done more reps than normal but needed more time to cool down.

If he went back to the kitchen, he would attack poor Stella. Fuck, he wanted her. She texted him yesterday like she said she would but made no mention of getting together again. Afraid of looking pathetic, he hadn't texted her again, even though he wanted desperately to see her again and not just for sex.

Liar.

Okay, so maybe the sex was a big part of it, but Stella was so damn hot. He couldn't stop thinking about her naked body and the way she moaned and cried his name when she climaxed. She was so soft and warm, and her luscious curves fit perfectly against his body. God, he wanted her badly.

His dick was hardening again. He gritted his teeth and did three more reps before lowering the weights bar onto the metal supports above him. He continued to lie on the weight bench, panting harshly as he stared at the ceiling. He couldn't stay in here forever. He needed to go and make small talk with Stella and pretend that he wasn't seconds away from tearing off her clothes and burying his dick in her warmth.

"Ford?"

He jumped and sat up, nearly braining himself on the weights bar as he stared at Stella. Oh, Jesus, she was wearing a shirt that showed off a heart-stopping amount of cleavage, and her jeans hugged every curve of her lower body. His dick throbbed, and his heart pounded so loudly he was certain she would hear it.

"Stella? What's wrong?"

She had the oddest look on her face, and when she spoke, her voice was low and husky with undeniable need. "I was watching you lift weights. You're so damn strong."

His gaze dropped to her cleavage again, and she took a hesitant step forward. "I want you."

"I want you too," he said.

She ran across the room and straddled the weight bench, crowding her lush body up against his as she kissed him hard on the mouth. Their tongues met, flicking and darting and tasting, and he groaned and crushed her against his body. She kissed her way down his neck as she licked and nipped at his flesh. He groaned again before reaching for the hem of her shirt. He yanked it over her head and inhaled sharply when he saw her full breasts in the bright red bra.

"Fuck," he breathed.

"You like?" she asked.

"God, yes," he said before pressing a kiss between her breasts. He licked the swell of one perfect breast before nipping lightly. She moaned and thrust her chest into his face. He flicked open the front clasp and smiled when her breasts spilled out into his waiting hands. He kneaded them gently, tugging on her nipples while she wiggled out of the bra and dropped it on the floor. He palmed her breast as she unbuttoned her jeans, grabbed his free hand, and shoved it down her pants.

"If you don't touch me right now, I'm going to scream," she said breathlessly.

He wiggled his hand past her panties to cup her pussy. He rubbed her clit. She was already wet and swollen, and she threw her arms around him and kissed him frantically. He pushed his index finger into her tight core, and she moaned and arched her back. He bent his head and sucked on one tight, pink nipple as she gasped and cried out. He stroked her clit almost roughly with his thumb, and she squeezed around his finger before riding his hand to a body-shaking climax.

"Oh fuck, that felt good," she gasped into his ear.

He kissed her neck and touched the thick braid of her hair. "I like making you feel good."

"Your turn," she said. "Help me get these jeans off."

She wiggled back, and he grabbed the waistband of her jeans. She braced her hands on the weight bench and lifted her hips.

"Jesus, why did I have to wear such tight pants," she muttered as he yanked them down her hips.

"I like them," he said hoarsely.

She giggled as he yanked again, and the tight denim slid down her thighs. He caught a flash of red silk as the denim dragged her panties with them.

"Dammit, you didn't even see the matching panties."

"You can show me later," he said as he peeled off her jeans and tossed them on the floor. Before he could stand, she had shoved down the front of his gym shorts and grasped his cock in her hand. He groaned, his head falling back as she bent and took the tip of him into her mouth. She sucked hard, and he wrapped his hand around her braid, holding tight as she sucked and licked. He stroked her smooth back and squeezed her ass as she sucked him and then made a harsh groan of disappointment when she suddenly straightened.

She licked her mouth and grinned at him. "Not in my mouth this time. I want to be fucked."

His nostrils flared, and he yanked her forward into his lap. His cock brushed against her stomach, and she reached between them and guided him into her hot core. He gripped her hips and pulled her closer, his cock sinking into her in one easy push. She moaned before kissing him again.

"So good," she breathed against his mouth.

"Yes," he said. "Are you too sore?"

She shook her head and squeezed his waist with her knees. He held her hips and pumped back and forth. The hot, wet slide of her pussy made him moan. He turned his face away as he thrust in and out. Her warm hand cupped his jaw, and she turned him back to face her before sucking on his lower lip.

He kissed her roughly, forcing his tongue past her lips as he moved harder and faster. When she let go of his jaw to slide her hand between their bodies, he turned his face away again. He stared at the wall, listening to the low slap of their bodies as she made a soft sigh.

"Ford, look at me."

He stared at her, and she smiled sweetly. "Don't look away from me. Please."

He held her gaze as she rubbed lightly at her clit. Her pussy tightened around him, and he made a harsh groan.

"Jesus, Stella, you're going to make me come."

"I like it when you come," she whispered. "I like it when you fuck me with your big dick, and I like it when you eat my pussy."

His whole body shuddered, and he thrust so deeply into her that the weight bench scraped along the floor.

"I especially like having your dick in my mouth," she said.

"Fuck!" The word exploded from his lungs. He made a harsh shout of pleasure as his balls tightened and his climax roared through him. Dimly, he was aware of her low cry as she brought herself to orgasm. He plastered her against his chest as her pussy clenched and unclenched around him. Panting, she collapsed against him, and he kissed the side of her neck as he stroked her naked back.

"If you promised me that every workout would end like this, I would be totally on board with daily exercise," she said.

He laughed, and she smiled at him. "God, I love your laugh."

They stared at each other for a moment before she smiled again. "Our coffees are getting cold."

Instead of letting her go, he held her a little closer. She put her arms around him and kissed him. "What are your plans for today?"

"I didn't have any."

"Me neither," she said.

There was a beat of silence, and she stared encouragingly at him.

"Do you want to hang out today?" he asked.

"Yes," she said. "I'd really like that."

"Me too. Have you had breakfast?"

She shook her head, and he squeezed her waist. "C'mon, I'll make you an omelet."

* * *

"Ford?" Stella pushed the last of her omelet around her plate with the tip of her fork.

"Yeah?"

"I like you."

"I like you too."

"No, I mean, I like you, and I want to date you."

His fork clattered to his plate, and she winced as he stared at her.

"I told myself to play it cool, not to be super clingy," she said, "but I wanted to see you last night. I don't want to play stupid games. I want to be with you."

"You want to date me," he said.

"Yes."

"You don't want to just have sex with me."

"Well, I want to have sex with you, but I also want to do other stuff too. Boyfriend/girlfriend stuff." She groaned. "Boyfriend/girlfriend stuff? Fuck, Stella, you sound like you're sixteen instead of twenty-six."

She pushed her plate away and gave him a small smile. "I know you like your space. You're quiet and an introvert, and I am the exact opposite of that, but we can make it work. Anytime we're together, and you need some time to yourself, tell me, and I'll bugger off for a few hours. I won't be hurt or upset. I promise."

"You want to be my girlfriend," he said in a low voice.

"Yes." She hesitated and then stood. "I'm going to leave and give you some time to think it over, okay? Just text me when, uh, whenever. Also, if you're not interested in dating, please be honest. I'm a big girl, and I can handle it. But I would still be up for having sex with you from time to time if you're, um, interested."

He didn't reply, and she smiled weakly before practically running to his exercise room. She had thrown on one of his shirts instead of getting dressed, and she grabbed her panties from her jeans and slid them over her hips.

"Could you be more pathetic, Stella?" she mumbled. "Hey, Ford, if you don't want to be my boyfriend, that's okay, but can we still have sex sometimes? Pretty please?"

She grunted in disgust and stripped off Ford's t-shirt. "I told you to play it cool, you dork. But no, you just had to throw it all out there after one night in Ford's bed. You just couldn't leave well enough alone."

She reached for her bra, shrieking when Ford's hands gripped her waist and turned her around.

"Ford?"

He cupped her ass, stroking the silky material of her panties before squeezing her ass cheeks. "I like your panties."

She laughed a bit breathlessly. "Thank you."

He lifted her, and she squeaked in surprise and wrapped her legs around his waist as he stared at her naked breasts. Without speaking, he turned and carried her out of the room.

"What are you doing?" she asked.

"Taking my girlfriend to the bedroom," he said.

Warmth rushed through her, and she threw her arms around his shoulders and hugged him before kissing him on the mouth. "What exactly will you do to your girlfriend in the bedroom, Mr. Taylor?"

He gave her a panty-melting grin, and her entire body shuddered when he said, "You're about to find out, Miss Stella."

CHAPTER 12

"Are you still coming to my place after work?" Ford asked.

Stella nodded. "Yes. What time is your dentist appointment?"

"Four, so I should be home by five-thirty at the latest."

"Do you want me to start supper?"

An odd look crossed his face, and she laughed and poked him in the arm. "Hey, I'm not that bad of a cook."

"You could make the salad."

"Sure," she said.

Ford stood and checked his watch. "I'd better go. I'm taking a short lunch to make up for leaving early." He hesitated, his gaze flickering to Jasmine, who sat across from them.

She grinned at him and bit into her pear, watching them both with bright interest. His cheeks red, Ford bent and gave Stella a brief kiss.

Her hand curled around his neck, stopping him from pulling away. "You can do better than that, big guy."

He smiled and gave her a longer, more thorough kiss before straightening. "I'll see you tonight."

"You bet, honey," she said.

She watched as he crossed the atrium and walked toward the security desk. "God, that man's ass," she said. "It is delightful."

"It is pretty fine," Jasmine said. "Have I mentioned how adorable you two are?"

"We are, aren't we?" Stella said.

Jasmine laughed. "How long have you been dating now?"

"It'll be two months tomorrow," Stella said. "Can you believe it?"

"That's so great, Stella. I'm happy for you."

"Thanks."

"Have you met his family yet?"

Stella shook her head. "No. I don't think Ford's close to them. I know they live here in the city, and his father owns an investment company. He has an older brother and a younger sister, but he doesn't talk about them."

"That's weird."

Stella shrugged. "It seems a little weird to me, too, but I'm probably closer to my family than most people. So, I may not have the best judgment regarding that sort of thing."

"Your family likes Ford?"

"They love him," Stella said. "I'm quite sure he likes them too. He's always up for hanging out with them, and my nephew Ethan thinks he's the greatest thing since sliced bread. Ford is good with him, so patient and sweet. He'll make a great father someday."

Jasmine studied her. "You love him, don't you?"

"Yes," Stella said. "I do."

"Have you told him?"

"No, not yet. He's so shy, and I'm starting to wonder if he's even had a girlfriend before. He's never mentioned any previous girlfriends. It's only been in the last few weeks that he hasn't pulled away or apologized for, like, holding my hand or cuddling when we watch TV."

Jasmine laughed. "Ford's into cuddling?"

"He totally is. He tries to pretend he isn't, but he's a big old teddy bear. I love it. My last boyfriend wasn't really into cuddling if he wasn't going to get sex from it, so I can't get enough of Ford's cuddling."

She munched on a raw carrot stick before smiling at Jasmine. "Enough about me and Ford. How are things going with Jimmy?"

"Good," Jasmine said. "We're going away this weekend. Jimmy's dad has a cabin up in the mountains, and it will be just my man and me for three whole days. I can't wait."

"That sounds like fun," Stella said. "I was thinking the four of us need to do another double date. What do you think?"

"I'd like that. Talk to Ford, and I'll talk to Jimmy, and maybe we can do something next weekend," Jasmine said.

Stella ate another carrot stick and smiled to herself. Things were going well with Ford, and she'd never been happier.

* * *

THE NEXT AFTERNOON, STELLA GRABBED HER USUAL TABLE IN the atrium and pulled out her book. Ford had texted her to say he had a brief errand to run during lunch, and she decided she would wait for him to return before eating. She sipped water from her water bottle and opened her book.

"Excuse me, is this seat taken?"

Stella looked up. The man standing next to her table in the atrium was devastatingly handsome.

"It isn't," she said.

He smiled with perfectly straight white teeth and sat down next to her. She studied his tanned skin and dark hair as his gaze wandered over her hair. "You have beautiful hair."

"Thanks," she said. "Do you work in the building?"

"No. I'm here visiting someone, but he doesn't seem to be here."

She glanced around the mostly empty atrium, wondering why the guy decided to sit at her table.

"My name's Dylan."

"Nice to meet you," she said as his gaze dipped to her chest before he smiled again.

Hey, Stella? He's hitting on you.

No fucking way.

Yes, fucking way.

The man smiled at her. "Are you going to tell me your name, gorgeous?"

"What are you doing here, Dylan?"

They both looked up at the sound of Ford's voice. Stella's welcoming smile died on her lips. Ford was holding a bouquet of flowers, but he was glaring at the man beside her.

"Hello, Ford," the man said.

"Wait, you two know each other?" Stella said.

"He's my brother," Ford said.

There was an awkward silence, and Stella said, "It's nice to meet you. I'm Stella, Ford's girlfriend."

Dylan's mouth dropped open, and he stared at her for so long that Ford made a low, angry snarl under his breath.

"You – you're Ford's girlfriend." His gaze turned to Ford, and Stella bristled at the look on his face.

"Yes, I am."

Dylan shook his head before grinning. "Funny joke, Ford. Good one."

Ford's face turned red. Stella glared at Dylan before pushing her chair back. She wrapped her arm around Ford's waist and took the bouquet from him. "Are these for me, honey?"

"Yeah," he said.

"For our anniversary?"

He nodded. His face was still red, and he was staring at the floor. Stella stood on her tiptoes and cupped his face before pressing her mouth against his. He grunted in surprise when she pushed her tongue into his mouth but returned her kiss.

She squeezed his waist and smiled at him. "They're beautiful. Thank you, honey. I love them."

"You're welcome," he said.

She rested her head against Ford's chest and gave his brother a brittle smile as Ford cleared his throat. "Why are you here, Dylan?"

"We haven't seen you since Christmas. Mother was... worried about you."

"I've been busy."

"Yes, I see that." Dylan's gaze drifted over Stella's body. Ford pulled her closer, his hand cupping her hip possessively.

"Ford usually drops by once a month for a family dinner," Dylan said to her. "It seems you've been distracting him."

"It has nothing to do with her," Ford said. "Tell Mother I'll come by Friday night."

Dylan stood and smoothed his suit jacket. "I will. Bring Stella."

"No," Ford said.

Dylan raised his eyebrows. "You don't want your *girlfriend* to meet your family? That seems odd."

Ford flushed again, and Stella said, "I would love to go. What time?"

"Stella," Ford said, "that isn't a -"

"Around six," Dylan said.

"See you then," Stella said.

Dylan nodded to her and walked away without looking at Ford.

"Jesus, what a dick," Stella said.

Ford jerked against her, and she said, "Sorry, honey. That's not a nice thing to say about your brother."

He didn't reply, and she squeezed his waist. "The flowers are really beautiful. Thank you for remembering our anniversary."

"It isn't a good idea for you to meet my family."

"Why not?" she said. "Are you embarrassed by me?"

"What? No!" he said. "My family isn't the nicest, and I don't want them upsetting you."

She shrugged. "You think I haven't heard a fat joke before? Don't worry, Ford, I have thick skin."

She sat down, laying the bouquet on the seat beside her. Ford was anxious. She could see it in the stiffness of his body as he dropped into the chair across from her. "Stella," he said, "I am perfectly okay with you not wanting to meet my family."

"But I do want to meet them," she said. "Honestly, they can't be that bad. You're wonderful, so they must have some good in them. Well, maybe not your brother, but I bet your mom and sister are super sweet."

"They're not," he said flatly.

"Ford?" Stella took his hand, trying not to wince when he gripped it hard. "Honey, if you don't want me to go, I won't."

She could hear the hurt in her voice. Ford's family couldn't be that bad, could they? It was more likely something to do with her. She had a temper, and she was outspoken. If his family were on the rude side, it wouldn't be unlike her to say something. Maybe if she promised Ford she'd behave and keep her mouth shut, it would make him feel better.

"I'll be on my best behaviour, I promise. But I'll understand if you don't want me to meet your family."

"It's not that, it's… I want you to come with me," he said.

She didn't quite believe him but smiled and tried to sound positive. "It'll be good. I promise."

* * *

STELLA STARED WORRIEDLY AT FORD. HE WAS PALE AND WHITE knuckling the steering wheel. She squeezed his arm as he turned into a residential area.

"Honey, it's going to be fine."

"Yeah, I know," he said. "We're here."

She looked up, and her jaw dropped. Ford was parking in the driveway of a damn mansion.

"This is your parents' house?" she said.

He nodded and shut off the truck.

"Holy crap. Don't take this wrong, but are your parents rich?"

"Yes."

"How rich? Filthy rich or moderately rich?"

A small smile crossed his face. "Filthy rich."

"Huh." Stella unbuckled her seat belt and smoothed down her skirt. "Well, let's go meet your filthy rich family."

A sick look crossed Ford's face, but he climbed out of the truck and moved to the passenger's side. She smiled as he lifted her down and squeezed his arms again. "You know you don't have to lift me out of the truck, right? You have a running board."

"I know," he said.

"You're just trying to cop a feel, aren't you?" She teased him gently, trying to ease some of the tension she could feel radiating from his body.

He didn't smile and she impulsively hugged him. "Honey, don't worry. Please."

He buried his face in her hair and threaded his fingers through it before kissing her briefly. "Your hair looks really pretty."

"Thank you," she said. "Are you ready?"

"Yeah." He didn't take her hand, and she frowned a little before reaching out and grabbing it. She squeezed it, and he held her hand in a death grip as they approached the front door.

They were still a few feet away when it opened, and an older man bent with age and wearing a dark suit stood in the doorway and smiled at them.

"Hello, Master Taylor."

Stella breathed a sigh of relief. Ford's grip had eased a little on her hand, and he smiled warmly.

"Hello, Henry." He hugged the older man before turning to Stella. "Stella, this is Henry. Henry, this is my, uh, girlfriend, Stella Johnson."

Henry held out his hand, and Stella shook it. "It's nice to meet you, Henry."

"It's wonderful to meet you, Ms. Johnson." Henry continued to hold her hand. "I'm so glad Master Taylor has brought you here."

"Ford, Henry," Ford said. "You know I hate the Master Taylor thing."

"Old habits die hard," Henry said with a grin. He still held Stella's hand and gave her another cheerful smile before tugging her into the house.

"How did you and Ford meet?" He took her jacket.

"We work in the same office building," she said.

"Lovely, just lovely." Henry couldn't stop grinning at her, and Stella could feel her own smile widening. It was obvious that Ford and Henry were very fond of each other. She took

Ford's hand again and squeezed it as Henry turned and put their jackets in the closet.

"I like him," she mouthed, and Ford smiled.

"Your siblings are already here and are in the family room with your parents," Henry said. "Go and introduce your lovely girlfriend to them."

He gave Ford an encouraging look. Gripping her hand so tightly her fingers tingled, Ford led her down the hallway.

"Honey, ease up a little," she said.

He loosened his grip. "I'm sorry."

"It's okay," she said as they entered a large room with a massive fireplace. Ford's family was gathered next to the corner bar, and she blinked in surprise. They were all gorgeous - like supermodel gorgeous. His mother was tall and thin with blonde hair in a carefully styled bob. Her bright blue eyes widened in surprise as she stared at Stella before her gaze turned to Ford's father.

Ford's father was giving Stella a stunned look of disbelief. She scanned his face, looking for any signs of Ford coming up empty. Dylan was the spitting image of his father – they looked like they had stepped directly out of a GQ magazine. For one brief, shameful moment, Stella wondered if Ford was adopted.

Ford's hand had tightened on hers again, and she glanced at him. His face was bloodless, and he looked like he was about to vomit. His family continued to stare wide-eyed at her. Stella was beginning to feel like a bug pinned to a board. An awkward silence filled the room, and she squeezed Ford's hand.

She cleared her throat when he didn't take the hint and said, "Hi there. I'm Stella Johnson, Ford's girlfriend."

The second blonde woman, Stella assumed it was Ford's sister, brayed harsh laughter before downing the amber liquid in her glass in one large swallow.

"Ford's girlfriend, right," she said.

Before Stella could reply, Ford walked toward his family, nearly dragging her with him. "Stella, this is my mother, Helen, and my father, Christopher."

"It's very nice to meet you," Stella said before holding out her hand.

Helen blinked at her before giving her a limp handshake. "Hello, Stella."

His father's handshake was cold and impersonal. He continued to stare at her without saying a word.

"You know Dylan," Ford said.

Stella smiled stiffly at his brother as Ford said, "This is my sister Suzanne."

"Hi, Suzanne. It's nice to meet you," Stella said.

"Sure," Suzanne said with a bitter smile. "What do you want to drink?"

"Oh, just water, please," Stella said.

"You don't drink?" Suzanne said.

"Not really."

"More for me," Suzanne said before turning away and pouring herself another glass.

Threads of disquiet crept down her spine as Stella glanced at Ford. He tried to smile at her, but it came out as a grimace. She smiled reassuringly at him even though she was starting to think that meeting his family was a bad idea – the worst idea in the world, in fact. She moved closer, and he dropped her hand and put his arm around her waist. His entire family tracked the movement, and she leaned into him as his parents glanced at each other.

"Why don't we sit down," his father said. He walked stiffly toward the couch, and after a moment, his wife and children followed him. They sat in a neat row on the sofa, looking like the world's perfect family. Stella swallowed the sudden and completely inappropriate laughter bubbling in her chest.

Ford still stood frozen next to the bar. She took his hand and led him to the loveseat across from the couch. He sat down. His wide bulk took up most of the room, and she squeezed in next to him, resting her hand on his large thigh and rubbing it. He put his arm around her, and she smiled at his family.

"Your home is beautiful, Mr. and Mrs. Taylor."

"Thank you," Helen said.

There was more silence. Her nerves beginning to fray, Stella said, "Was this your childhood home, Ford?"

He grunted out a yes.

"I'm jealous," Stella said. "My house was quite a bit smaller. I had to share a room with my sister until she moved out."

There was no response from his family. Stella could feel sweat beading on her forehead. Ford's family seemed to be as introverted as he was. The thought of carrying the conversation for the entire night made her stomach churn.

"So, uh, Dylan, I know you work with your father," she said, "but do you work for the family business as well, Suzanne?"

"I'm a lawyer." Suzanne tossed back the rest of her drink.

"Oh, good for you. Do you have your own practice?"

"No. How did you and Ford meet?"

Stella smiled at Ford and squeezed his thigh again. "We work in the same building."

"You work at the mall?" Christopher asked.

"I – I'm sorry?" Stella said.

"You work at the mall with Ford?"

"Uh, no," Stella said before staring at Ford.

"Dad, I don't work security at the mall," Ford said. "I work in an office building downtown."

"Right," Christopher said. "So, you work security as well?"

"No," Stella said. "I work in admin for a –"

"How long have you been dating?" Suzanne said.

"Two months," Stella said.

"You've been dating a woman for two months and didn't tell us," Suzanne said to Ford. "Are you ashamed of us?"

"No," Ford said.

"I should hope not." Suzanne walked to the bar and poured herself another drink. She took a large swallow, grimaced, and stared shrewdly at Stella. "So, why exactly are you dating my brother? We know it's not his charming personality or," her gaze lingered on Ford's face, "his good looks, so why exactly would someone who looks like you be dating him?"

"Excuse me?" Stella's cheeks flushed, and her pulse raced as anger rushed through her. She ignored Ford when he squeezed her shoulder with his hand. "What did you just say?"

"Stella," Ford said in a low voice, "don't -"

"Dinner is ready." Henry entered the room and crossed to Ford and Stella. He held out his arm to Stella. "Perhaps I could escort you to the dining room, Stella."

She took a deep breath and forced herself to smile at him. "Thank you, Henry. I'd like that."

* * *

THE DINING ROOM WAS LARGE, LAVISHLY DECORATED, AND oddly cold and impersonal despite the family photos on the wall. Stella murmured her thanks to Henry when he pulled out her chair for her. Ford sat beside her, and she watched silently as his parents and siblings sat down. His mother was sitting on Ford's right side, and she took a quick glance at him. Stella scowled when a small, pained look of disgust crossed her face before she looked hastily away.

The food was already on the table, and the Taylors

silently dished it onto their plates. It looked and smelled delicious, but Stella's throat had closed to roughly the size of a pinhole, and she had lost what little appetite she'd had. She studiously avoided looking at Suzanne, and as Ford pushed the food around on his plate while his family ate silently, she studied the photos that hung on the walls.

There were photos of Dylan and Suzanne, both as adults and as children. There were also a few pictures of Helen and Christopher on the beach, looking tanned and relaxed. There was a photo collage of Dylan with a dark-haired woman and two young boys and a photo of a much younger Suzanne in a graduation gown and laughing into the camera. Stella scanned the images, fresh irritation flooding through her when she realized there wasn't a single picture of Ford.

Hanging on the far wall of the dining room was a large pencil-drawn portrait of Christopher and Helen sitting on chairs in front of the family room fireplace. Dylan and Suzanne were posed behind them with their hands resting on their parents' shoulders. The detail in the portrait was amazing, and she felt a swell of pride. Ford obviously had drawn it.

"That portrait of the family is stunning, Mrs. Taylor. You must be enormously proud of Ford," Stella said before taking a small bite of salad.

Helen stared blankly at her. "I'm sorry?"

Ford was shaking his head. Stella stared at him in confusion before pointing to the picture. "The portrait Ford drew. You must be proud of his artistic ability."

Dylan leaned forward and stared in surprise at Ford. "You still draw?"

"Don't be silly, Dylan," Helen said. "Of course, Ford doesn't still draw. He's not the artist type."

"He is an artist," Stella said. "How can you not know that?"

Helen flushed. "As a child, he was always going off on his own and drawing pictures, but I'd hardly say that makes him an artist."

"Maybe if you had spent less time with your nose in a sketch pad and more time on your education, you would be working in the family business instead of mall security," Christopher said to Ford.

"He doesn't work at a mall," Stella said, "and he's an amazing artist. I've seen his work, and it's incredible."

"I doubt that," Suzanne said.

Anger coursing through her veins, Stella glared icily at Suzanne before turning to stare at Helen. "Why are there no pictures of Ford?"

"Stella, it doesn't matter," Ford said. "Let's just eat and -"

"I want to know," Stella said. "Where are the pictures of Ford?"

Helen cleared her throat. "Ford isn't exactly photogenic, Ms. Johnson."

Stella's mouth dropped open. When her hand curled into a fist around her butter knife, Ford hurriedly pried open her hand and took the knife from her.

"He's your son," she said. "You should have pictures of him."

"You think you can come into my house and tell me what to do? You think just because you're dating my son that you know -"

"Please, Mother," Suzanne said, "don't encourage the charade."

"What's that supposed to mean?" Stella said.

Suzanne rolled her eyes. "It means we all know that you're not actually dating Ford, and trying to convince us that you are is both stupid and pathetic."

"Enough, Suzanne," Ford said in a low growl.

"You could have at least picked someone ugly to be your

fake girlfriend," Suzanne said. "We might have considered that you'd found someone to sleep with you if she was ugly."

The blood drained from Ford's face, and hot rage overtook Stella. She stood and glared at Ford's family.

"What is wrong with all of you?" she said. "This is your son, your brother, and you're treating him like he's a piece of garbage."

Christopher glared at her. "You have no right to -"

"Shut up!" Stella shouted as Ford stood and tried to take her hand.

"Stella, let's go."

She shook him off angrily. "Ford is a good man. In fact, he's the best man I know, and I won't sit here and listen to you talk shit about him. He's better than all of you put -"

"You don't know anything about us," Suzanne said. "So just keep your mouth -"

"You can shut the fuck up as well!" Stella snarled. "You think you're better than your brother, but you're wrong. You're a garbage-spewing piece of shit, and you should be ashamed of yourself."

She studied each of them with contempt. "You should all be ashamed. I've been here for less than an hour, and it's already perfectly clear that you have no idea who Ford is. You treat him like shit because of the way he looks and -"

"You don't know what you're talking about," Christopher said.

"Like fuck I don't!" Stella shouted. Her entire body shook, and she gripped the table's edge as she leaned forward and stared at the others. She was being irrationally angry. Somewhere inside of her, she recognized that fact, but it wasn't enough to stop her.

After months of watching how strangers reacted to Ford's appearance and treated him like he was a monster –finding out that his family did the same thing to him brought her anger and her hurt for Ford to a boil. It spilled out of her in a raging rush of hatred.

"How you look at Ford and treat him makes me sick!" she shouted. "You think you're better than him because of how you look? You're ugly inside and out, and not one of you is half the person that Ford is. You don't deserve to know the real Ford, and I hope you all choke on your goddamn dinner. You're nothing but a – a bunch of vile, repulsive inbred hillbillies!"

There was a moment of shocked silence, and then Suzanne, with her hand clenched around her glass of liquor, said, "So how much is my brother paying you to pretend to be his girlfriend?"

Stella lunged across the table at her with a low, inarticulate snarl of rage. Helen screamed as Suzanne jerked back. Her chair tipped over, and she fell on the floor, her drink spilling across her face and shirt as Ford grabbed Stella around the waist. She struggled furiously, but he lifted her and carried her out of the room.

Henry was waiting for them by the front door, and he watched with a small smile as Ford carried the cursing, struggling Stella down the hall.

"Your jackets, Master Taylor," he said as he held them out.

Ford grabbed them with one hand as Stella glared at him. "You let me go right now, Ford Taylor!"

"It's time to leave," Ford said as Henry opened the door.

"We'll leave as soon as I punch your bitch of a sister in the face!" Stella shouted.

Henry made a muffled snort of laughter, and Ford cursed with pain when Stella kicked him hard in the shin. He set her down and rubbed at his shin. Henry laughed again when Stella immediately turned and bolted toward the dining room. Ford chased after her. He caught her easily, and she shouted in outrage when he heaved her over his shoulder and marched back to the front door.

"Put me down, Ford!" She pounded on his broad back with her fists.

He ignored her and stepped outside. Henry trailed after them with a wide grin on his wrinkled face as Ford carried her wiggling body to the truck, her mouth spitting curses the entire way.

"It was so wonderful to meet you, Ms. Johnson. I do hope you'll visit again soon," Henry called as Ford put her in the truck. "Good night, Ford."

"Bye, Henry," Ford grunted before slamming her door shut, climbing behind the wheel, and driving away.

CHAPTER 13

Her hands shaking and feeling sick to her stomach, Stella glanced again at Ford. He was staring out the windshield, gripping the steering wheel tightly. She opened her mouth to apologize before shutting it. She had tried to apologize not two minutes ago, and without looking at her, he shook his head briefly.

Away from Ford's family, it hadn't taken long for her anger to dissipate, and she was immediately ashamed of her behaviour. She stared at her trembling hands, wondering if Ford would even bother to tell her he was dumping her or just drop her off at her house and never speak to her again.

She blinked back the hot tears. What had she been thinking?

She hadn't thought that was the problem. Her temper got the best of her like it so often did, and she lashed out at Ford's horrible family on impulse.

They deserved it.

Yeah, they did deserve it. But as awful as they were to Ford, they were still his family, and she had made an absolute fool of herself in front of them. Ford was a grown man and

177

fully capable of taking care of himself, and she should never have said the things she did.

Don't forget when you tried to kill his sister.

She groaned inwardly and clenched her hands together in a tight fist. She had tried to punch his sister.

His sister!

Even if Ford could forgive her for losing her shit and screaming at his family, he'd never forgive her for trying to harm Suzanne physically – even if Suzanne was an asshole.

Okay, Stella, so you fucked up royally. The only thing left to do is beg for Ford's forgiveness when he tries to dump your ass. Promise you'll never do it again – promise him a thousand blowjobs – just do whatever you need to do. Ford's the best thing that's ever happened to you, and you know it.

Ford shut off the truck, and she glanced up, surprised to see that they were at his house. She had expected him to take her to her house, and she stared tentatively at him as he opened the door and slid out of the truck. He didn't come to her side to lift her from the truck. Hell, he didn't even wait for her - just walked quickly to the front door - and her heart sank. Over the last month or so, she had left a few things at his house - toiletries and extra clothes. He obviously brought her here first to get them out of his house.

Her stomach rolling and pulse thudding erratically, she climbed out of the truck and walked slowly toward his house. He had already opened the front door and disappeared, and she took a deep breath before entering the dark hallway.

You can still fix this, Stella. Just be calm, explain why you did what you did, and then apologize again. Ford will understand.

She squinted in the dim light. Ford hadn't turned on the hallway light and she could just make out his big body standing a few feet away from her. But it was easy to tell that his fists were clenched, and his shoulders were hunched. She swiped at the tears sliding down her cheeks as she shut the front door.

"Ford?" she said tentatively, hating how her voice hitched. "I'm very sorry. I shouldn't have lost my temper like that. I know you're angry with me, but I promise you that I -"

Ford stomped toward her, and her words were cut off with a startled squeak when he pushed her up against the wall and kissed her roughly.

She gasped when his big hands grabbed the front of her shirt and pulled. Buttons flew off and scattered on the tile floor at their feet. She moaned when he pushed down the cups of her bra and sucked one nipple into his mouth. He nipped at it, worrying it with his teeth and lips until it was a hard peak as his fingers pinched and pulled at her other nipple. She moaned again, her hands burying in his hair to pull up his head.

"Ford, wh-what are you doing?"

He stared at her, and the dark lust on his face sent an immediate answering throb through her body.

"Ford?" she whispered.

He shoved her skirt up around her waist, grabbed her panties, and yanked. They ripped with a low purring sound, and he tossed them aside as he shoved her legs apart with one muscular thigh. His hand pressed between her legs, his rough fingers finding her clit and rubbing hard as he threaded his fingers through her long hair and pulled her head back. He kissed her throat before biting her. The slight and unexpected pain sent another pulse of lust through her lower body and a gush of wetness to her pussy.

He groaned at the rush of liquid against his fingertips and sucked at her nipple again before fumbling at his belt. He unbuckled it and unbuttoned his jeans, shoving them and his briefs down his legs. His erect cock was huge, and the tip a dark red. It stood straight up to brush against his lower abdomen. She reached down and stroked him lightly.

He groaned again and grabbed both her arms, yanking them above her head and pinning them to the wall with one hand as his other arm wrapped around her waist. He lifted her. She automatically parted her legs around his waist, and they both moaned when his cock rubbed against her pussy. He lifted her a little higher and pinned her to the wall with his lower body before reaching between them and guiding his cock to her entrance. He slammed into her, his cock pushing past the slight resistance of her pussy as she cried his name.

He thrust roughly, his hand still pinning her arms above her head and his pelvic bone grinding against her clit with every thrust. She gasped and moaned. Her body shook as he licked and nipped at her throat and upper chest. Her sensitive nipples rubbed against his chest hair, and the sensation sent beats of pleasure through her body. Ford had never been so rough with her, and she was a little surprised by how hot it made her. She was already close to coming.

Ford released her arms and gripped her thighs. He held her steady as he pounded into her, and she wrapped her arms around his neck and held tight. He buried his face in her throat, his breath coming in harsh gasps as he plunged in and out.

Her orgasm was starting. Her stomach was a tight coil, and her entire body was shaking against his. He drove her higher and higher, each relentless thrust of his cock stoking the fire inside of her until the flame consumed her. She screamed as she climaxed, her pussy tightening around him and holding his cock deep inside of her as the pleasure exploded in her body.

He shouted her name, and his fingers dug into her thighs as he pinned her against the wall with his cock and came.

Every muscle in his body clenched as she squeezed compulsively around him. He drove in and out for a few more earth-shattering strokes until he groaned and slowed to a stop.

His hands relaxed their grip, and he stroked her thighs as he kept his face buried in her throat. She rubbed his back tentatively through his shirt before whispering, "Ford?"

He pulled out of her and eased her to her feet, then hauled up his briefs and jeans. He picked her up and carried her to the bedroom. He tugged off her skirt. He removed her ruined shirt and stared blankly at the ripped material before discarding it on the floor and removing her bra. He stripped off his clothes and guided Stella to the bed. Her legs were still shaking, and she climbed unsteadily into bed as Ford joined her on the other side. He pulled her into his embrace, pushing her head down onto his chest and running his hand over her hair.

"Ford?" Stella said.

"I'm sorry for ruining your shirt," he said.

She sat up, pushing away his hands when he tried to keep her in his arms. "You're sorry?"

He flinched and sat up, leaning against the headboard. "Yes, and I'm sorry for being so rough."

She reached out and cupped his face. "Why are you not kicking me out?"

"Why would I kick you out?"

"Because I… because I screamed at your family. I called them inbred hillbillies, and I tried to beat up your sister. I'm the one who needs to apologize to you. I'm so sorry I lost my temper with your family. I'm sorry that I tried to punch your sister in the face. Please forgive me."

He laughed, and her mouth dropped open as she hugged her knees to her chest. "What is happening? I thought you were dumping me, and instead you – you fucked me into the best orgasm of my life."

"I didn't hurt you, did I?" He scanned her body, cursing under his breath at the red marks on her thighs.

"No," she said. "I just told you – it was the best orgasm of my life. Why are you not angry with me?"

"Stella," he reached out and cupped her face, "the way you stood up to my family and told them how awful they were – it was amazing."

"You're not mad at me?"

"Of course not."

"But you wouldn't talk to me at all on the drive home. You wouldn't even look at me," she said.

"Because I would have pulled the truck over and fucked you right there if I had looked at you," he said. "As it was, I could barely wait until you were in the house."

Her mouth dropped open. "Are you telling me that watching me shout at your family and threaten to beat up your sister was a turn-on for you?"

He laughed again. "Honestly, I'm starting to think that everything you do is a turn-on for me."

He rubbed his thumb across her lower lip. She took his hand and squeezed it. "I shouldn't have screamed at your family like that. I'm sorry."

He pulled her into his lap and cupped her face again, staring solemnly at her. "No one has ever defended me before like that. All my life, my mother and father and my siblings have treated me like I was nothing. They treated me like I was their burden to bear, and I accepted it because they're the only family I have. I love them, but I'm not stupid or hopeful enough to ever think they'll return that love."

He suddenly smiled. "But it doesn't matter now. I don't need them to love me or accept me. Because I have you, and I lo -"

He stopped, his face flushing bright red as he dropped his

hand from her face and lowered his gaze until he stared at her lap. She cupped his face and forced him to look at her.

"Say it, Ford," she whispered.

He swallowed, and she could hear the dry click of his throat. "I love you, Stella."

"I love you too," she said.

"You don't have to say -"

"Don't you dare, Ford Taylor," she said. "Don't you dare ruin this moment by pretending I'm only saying it because I think you want me to. You *know* that isn't true."

She pressed a light kiss against his mouth. "You *know* I love you. Admit it."

"I know you love me," he said.

She laughed and kissed him again. "I love you so much, Ford Taylor."

He hugged her and pressed kisses against her warm throat. "I love you too, Stella Johnson."

She relaxed in his arms as he stroked her long hair silently.

"What do we do about your family?" she asked.

"What do you mean?"

"I'm pretty sure I won't be invited to any more family dinners."

He laughed. "I don't care if I never see them again."

She sat up and stared searchingly at him. "You can go over there without me. I'll understand. I mean, they suck, and I hate them, but they are your family."

He laughed again before hugging her. "No, you're my family, Stella. You're the only one I need."

* * *

STELLA WAS ALONE AT FORD'S HOUSE SUNDAY MORNING WHEN the doorbell rang. She answered, smiling in surprise at

Henry standing on the front stoop. "Henry! It's so nice to see you again."

"It's nice to see you too, Miss Johnson," Henry said.

"Come in, please."

He followed her into the house, and she took his jacket. "Ford's at the grocery store, but he shouldn't be long. Can I offer you a cup of coffee or tea?"

"Tea would be wonderful, thank you, Miss Johnson."

"Call me Stella." She led him to the kitchen.

He sat at the table, and she made them both cups of tea before joining him. "I need to apologize to you, Henry."

"For what?"

"For my behaviour on Friday night. I'm not normally such a terrible dinner guest, I promise."

Henry laughed and sipped at his tea. "Stella, you have nothing to apologize for. The way you stood up for Master Taylor was courageous and enjoyable to witness."

She blushed a little, and Henry patted her hand. "Forgive my nosiness, but are you in love with Ford?"

"Yes," Stella said. "He loves me too."

"I'm not surprised. You're wonderful," Henry said.

Her blush deepened. "Ford's the wonderful one, not me."

"He is pretty amazing," Henry said. "You have no idea how happy I am that he's finally found love."

"How long have you worked for Ford's family?"

"A long time," he said. "So long I don't quite remember. I think Ford was five when I started working for Mr. Taylor."

"What was he like as a child?"

"Quiet," Henry said. "A bit withdrawn, but one can't blame him for that. His parents and his siblings were difficult."

Stella stared at him in horror. "Tell me they weren't that cruel to him when he was a child."

Henry didn't reply, and Stella dropped her gaze to her steaming cup of tea. "Oh my God. They really are monsters."

Henry patted her hand. "They weren't horrific to him, Stella. They mostly ignored him. Master Taylor tried very hard to win over his family, especially his mother, but she never warmed to him like she did his brother and sister."

"Never warmed to him?" Stella said. "He was her child. Did she – did any of them show him any affection or love?"

"No," Henry said.

"Did she tuck him in at night? Take care of him when he was sick? Did she do anything that a mom is supposed to do?"

Henry shook his head and Stella bit her trembling bottom lip as tears flowed down her cheeks. "I keep imagining Ford as a child. How awful it must have been for him."

"He did know love, Miss Johnson."

"You," she said.

Henry nodded. "I was a poor substitute for a father, but I did love him. When he was a child, I encouraged his love for drawing and bought him art supplies. When he joined the Boy Scouts, I went on the father/son camping trips with him. I watched his football games in high school, and when he won an art award, I attended the ceremony. I couldn't be there for him for everything he needed, but I tried. I never had a child, and I think of Ford as my son."

He sighed deeply. "When Ford was twelve, his parents took him to several plastic surgeons. They all refused to do surgery on someone so young. When he was eighteen, they tried again, but Ford refused to cooperate. He joined the military without telling them and left home."

"What is wrong with them?" Stella said.

"Ford's parents had a vision of what their life would look like. The perfect home, the perfect career, and the perfect family. Unfortunately, what other people think of them is particularly important to them. With his unconventional looks, Ford made them believe he had ruined their perfect life."

"That's not Ford's fault!"

"No, it isn't," Henry said. "His family aren't bad people, Stella."

"Do you really believe that?" she said.

"I *want* to believe it," Henry said.

"They are bad people," Stella said. "They're horrible and evil, and I hope they burn in hell for what they've done to Ford."

She started to cry again, and Henry patted her hand. "I'm sorry, Stella. I didn't come here to upset you."

She squeezed the older man's hand. "I'm glad you were there for him, Henry. Ford loves you very much."

They sat in silence for a few minutes while Stella composed herself. She blew her nose and washed her hands before sitting beside him again.

"I have a confession to make," Henry said. "I came here today in the hopes that I would have the chance to speak to you privately."

"Well, talk quickly," Stella said with a small smile. "Ford will be back soon."

"Ford is one of the toughest men I've ever met. He has to be to deal with his family and how strangers treat him. But he's also very fragile in a certain sense. He – he's sensitive, and his family's constant rejection has hurt him deeply. He won't admit it, but it has."

Henry sipped at his tea, his eyes watering a little. "He's never had anyone stand up for him before, and what you did on Friday night was amazing. It showed him that there are people in this world who don't judge him for his looks. Even if things don't work out with the two of you, what you did has forever changed him. Do you understand that, Stella?"

"I think so," Stella said as more tears dripped down her face.

"But he's spent his entire life being rejected for nothing more than how he looks, and something like that scars a man. Even a man as tough as Ford. I believe a part of him will never genuinely believe that a woman like you could love him for who he is. There may come a time when that doubt and that fear overcome his love for you, and he'll push you away."

Henry leaned forward and took Stella's hand again. "Don't let him push you away, Stella. Don't let his fears and insecurities ruin your love for each other. I know we've only met, and it's a lot for me to ask, but I love Ford and want him to be happy. You make him happy. Will you promise that when Ford tries to walk away, you'll stay strong and not let him leave?"

The front door slammed, and Ford shouted, "Stella, I'm back!"

"Will you promise me?" Henry said in a low voice.

Stella nodded. "I promise, Henry."

He squeezed her hand and quickly swiped his hand across his eyes as Ford entered the kitchen. "Stella, are you – Henry? What are you doing here?"

"I was close by and thought I'd stop in for a visit," Henry said as Ford studied Stella.

"Honey? What's wrong? Why are you crying?" he said.

Stella stood and hugged him. "There's nothing wrong. Did you get the pancake mix?"

He nodded. "I did. Are you sure you're okay?"

"Never better. Henry, will you stay and have brunch with us?" Stella said.

"I would love to," Henry said. "I'm anxious to get to know the girl who has stolen Ford's heart."

Ford blushed, and Stella stood on her tiptoes and kissed

his cheek. "You heard the man. Get cooking while I spill my life story."

* * *

"Those are wonderful, Stella," Jasmine said.

"Thanks, Jasmine." Stella shuffled through the pictures she had printed. After Sunday's brunch, she convinced Henry and Ford to let her take a few photos of them. She had them developed Tuesday night and was thrilled with how they turned out. She decided to grab some frames after work tonight and frame some for both Ford and Henry.

"Ford looks happy." Jasmine leaned over the counter and studied the pictures. "This will sound stupid, but I never noticed how pretty Ford's eyes are. The blue is a gorgeous shade."

Stella grinned at her. "Stay away from my man, Jazzy girl."

Jasmine laughed. "I have my hands full with Jimmy, trust me."

"You love every minute of it." Jimmy wandered into the flower shop. He glanced at the pictures. "Who's the old geezer with Ford?"

Stella punched him lightly on the arm. "His name is Henry, and he's a good friend of Ford's."

"Where is Ford anyway?" Jasmine asked. "Your lunch break is almost over."

"He had to run an errand," Stella said. "He should be back soon."

She studied the pictures again as Jimmy leaned over the counter and kissed Jasmine. "We still on for dinner with my parents tonight?"

"I thought they weren't back from the cabin yet?" Jasmine said.

"They came back a day early. There's supposed to be one

hell of a snowstorm this weekend, but Dad didn't want to get caught in it. Did you make other plans? I can text Mom and let her know we can't make it."

"Nope, that's fine," Jasmine said. "I just need to do a quick delivery after work."

"Stella?"

Stella swung around, the smile on her lips dying when she saw Ford's face. "Ford? Honey, what's wrong?"

Ford's face was white, and he swallowed compulsively as she hurried forward. "Dylan just texted me. Henry is in the hospital. He collapsed at the house, and they rushed him to the hospital by ambulance. I'm sorry, I can't have lunch with you. I need to go to the hospital."

"I'll come with you," Stella said. "Just give me a minute to run upstairs and let my boss know."

"You don't have to," Ford said hoarsely. "I don't want you getting in trouble at work, and I -"

Stella reached up and cupped his face. "Honey, stop. I'm coming with you. Okay?"

A look of relief crossed his face. "Okay, thank you."

She pressed a quick kiss against his mouth. "I'll be right back."

* * *

DYLAN WAS IN THE WAITING ROOM OF THE EMERGENCY ROOM when they arrived. He was pale, and his hands shook as he held the paper cup of coffee.

"How is he?" Ford asked.

"It's not good," Dylan said. "They don't think he's going to make it."

His voice broke, and he blinked rapidly before turning away from them. He tossed his coffee into the trash and blew his nose loudly. When he turned around, his eyes were still watering. He wiped them with a tissue before clearing his throat.

"What happened?" Ford said.

"They think he had a stroke. Mother said he wasn't looking very good when he came to the house this morning. She made him lie down in one of the guest rooms for a couple of hours. He got up and said he was feeling better, so Mother made him a cup of tea and a bowl of soup. He started eating and then Mother said he just – just grabbed his head and fell off the chair. She called 9-1-1."

Dylan's voice broke again, and he began to cry in earnest. Ford reached out to hug him, and Dylan pulled away from him, his face twisting. "Don't, Ford. I'm fine."

He suddenly scowled at Stella. "What are you doing here? You don't even know Henry. You don't even…"

He wiped at the tears on his cheeks. "She shouldn't be here, Ford."

"I'm here for Ford, and I'm not leaving," Stella said.

"Yeah, well, maybe if you could not threaten to punch anyone, that would be great," Dylan said.

Stella flushed but didn't say anything. Ford squeezed her hand. "Be quiet, Dylan. It isn't the time. I want to see Henry."

"They just moved him up to the intensive care unit," Dylan said. "Mother and Father and Suzanne are with him. Visitors are limited, so maybe you and your girlfriend should come back another time."

"Not a chance," Ford said. "Take me there right now, Dylan."

"He's not conscious. There's no need for you -"

"Take me to him!" Ford shouted.

Dylan flinched and took a step back. "Okay, fine. Just calm down, Ford. Jesus."

He started toward the elevators, and Ford and Stella followed silently.

* * *

STELLA STARED AT THE HALF-FINISHED PUZZLE IN FRONT OF her. It was just after nine, and she had been in the waiting room outside of the intensive care unit for hours. There was a pile of magazines, books, and boxes of puzzles, and she'd started a puzzle to have something to keep her brain occupied. Ford had come out every couple of hours to give her updates and to urge her to go home, but she'd refused.

She had seen Henry once when Ford's family left to eat dinner. Ford brought her into the room, and she held Henry's hand and tried to reassure Ford he would be fine. It wasn't easy to sound confident. The older man looked terrible. His skin was grey, and his body was hooked up to so many machines that there was barely any space to stand in the small room.

She added another piece to the puzzle and looked up in time to see Ford's father and mother walking past the waiting room. They didn't look her way, nor did Dylan. Suzanne glared at her as she passed, and Stella quickly looked away.

"Stella?"

Ford entered the waiting room, and she stood and hugged him. He rested his chin on top of her head. "How is he?"

"The same," Ford said. "Everyone's going home to get some sleep, but I'm going to stay. I don't want to leave him alone."

"That's fine," Stella said. "I'll stay with you."

"No," Ford said. "You've been here for hours, and I know you're tired. Go home and get some sleep."

"No," she said. "I'm not leaving you alone, Ford."

"Stella -"

"No," she repeated. "Don't ask me to leave you, honey. I can't."

He hugged her so tightly that she squeaked in protest. He released her and pressed a kiss against her forehead. "Thank you."

* * *

"MR. TAYLOR?"

Stella blinked sleepily and sat up as Ford shifted against her. They were crammed into a chair in Henry's room, and she stared blurrily at the man standing in the room.

"Yes?" Ford lifted Stella off his lap and stood.

"My name is Dr. Mirken. I'm Henry's family doctor."

"It's nice to meet you," Ford said before shaking his hand. "This is Stella Johnson."

The doctor nodded to her, and Stella gave him a brief smile before checking her cell phone. It was almost eight in the morning. She stretched the kinks out of her neck as the doctor stared gravely at Ford.

"I've looked over the test results for Henry, and I'm afraid the news isn't good."

"Did he have a stroke?" Ford said.

"Yes. Unfortunately, the tests show no activity in the brain," Dr. Mirken said.

"What – what do you mean?" Ford asked.

The fear in his voice broke Stella's heart, and she crowded up against him, putting her arm around his waist and hugging him.

"Henry is brain dead. I'm so sorry," Dr. Mirken said. "The only thing keeping him alive is the machines."

Ford stared blankly at him. "There has to be something else we can do."

"There isn't," Dr. Mirken said gently. "I'm sorry, but Henry isn't going to recover from this."

"He has to," Ford said. "People have strokes, and they – they get better with rehab and…"

He stared plaintively at the doctor. "He can get better."

"Henry's seventy-nine years old, Mr. Taylor," Dr. Mirken said. "The stroke was a massive one, and without these machines, he won't survive."

"We can give it some more time," Ford said. "Maybe in a few days or a few weeks -"

"Henry has a DNR order," Dr. Mirken said. "It states that he does not wish to be kept on life support."

Ford stared at Stella, and she rubbed his back as he said, "So what? We take him off the machines and let him die?"

Dr. Mirken nodded. "That's what Henry requested."

"Fuck," Ford said. His big hands clenched into fists, and he didn't seem to notice when Stella took one fist and massaged it open.

"I'm sorry. I know this is difficult," Dr. Mirken said. "Henry has you listed as his next of kin. I wanted to confirm with you that he has no blood relatives."

Ford shook his head. "He doesn't have any family left. He had a brother, but he died about seven years ago. It's just me and my family."

"As the next of kin, you'll need to make the final decision about taking him off life support," Dr. Mirken said.

Ford stared wide-eyed at him. "What?"

"You make the final decision," Dr. Mirken repeated. "Again, I know it's difficult, but please remember that Henry does have a DNR, and he was very specific about not being kept on life support if there was no chance of recovery."

"Are you sure he won't get better?" Ford asked.

"I'm positive. The EEG shows no brain activity. There's nothing to be done for Henry. I'm sorry."

"Stella?" Ford's voice was thin and tinged with panic. "What do I do?"

She hugged him. "I think you should honour Henry's wishes, honey."

He closed his eyes for a moment before nodding. "We'll take him off life support."

"You're making the right decision," Dr. Mirken said.

"I need to call Father. They need to say goodbye," Ford said.

"I can call them. You stay with Henry," Stella said. "Give me your cell phone, and I'll call them."

Ford handed her his phone, and she kissed his cheek before leaving the room.

* * *

"WHY DOES HE GET TO MAKE THE DECISION?" SUZANNE demanded. "Henry is just as important to us as he is to Ford. We should have a say in this."

"You don't," Dr. Mirken said. "I'm sorry, but Ford has been listed as the next of kin, which makes it his decision."

"What if he gets better, Ford?" Christopher said. "Are you okay with killing him when there was a chance he could recover?"

Ford winced, and Stella tried not to glare at his father. She rubbed Ford's back as Dr. Mirken said, "He won't get better. He's brain dead, and the only thing keeping him alive are these machines. As I mentioned, Henry has a very specific DNR order."

Ford's mother was weeping steadily, and Ford reached out. "Mom, I'm sorry. I didn't -"

"Don't touch me!" she snarled.

He jerked his hand away as Helen allowed Dylan to fold her into his embrace. She buried her face in his chest, and he kissed the top of her head before leading her to Christopher.

"Ford, are you ready?" Dr. Mirken asked.

Ford nodded, and all of them crowded around Henry's bed. He leaned over Henry and kissed his forehead before picking up his hand. He held it tightly as he put his other arm around Stella's waist.

Tears flowing down her face, Stella took a quick peek at Ford's family. All of them were weeping openly, but despite their obvious sorrow, she didn't feel sorry for them. She tried to feel some glimmer of sympathy, but it was buried by the hateful looks they shot Ford's way. As Dr. Mirken and a nurse shut off the machines, she slid her arms around Ford's waist and held him.

CHAPTER 14

"How is Ford doing?" Zoe asked.

Stella sighed as she dropped into the kitchen chair. "Not great. He won't talk about it, to be honest. I know he misses Henry, but he won't open up to me about it. I don't know what to do."

"Well, Ford isn't much of a talker," Jocelyn said as Stella held her arms out for Julie.

She handed the baby over, and Julie made a cooing noise of delight before resting her head on Stella's chest. Stella kissed the top of her head and inhaled her sweet scent as she rocked her.

"I know. I just – I'm worried about him. The funeral is tomorrow, and I don't think he's been sleeping very much lately. His family is still pissed that he took Henry off life support, and they refused to let him help with any of the arrangements."

"Are you going to the funeral with him?" Zoe asked.

"Yes. I took the day off work."

"Good, he needs you right now," Zoe replied. "Where is Ford?"

"He's at his place. He hasn't stayed over at my place since Henry died and hasn't asked me to stay with him. I asked him to join us for dinner, but he said he wanted to be alone." Stella stared at her mother. "Am I doing the right thing in leaving him alone, Mom? He's an introvert, and I promised him that if he ever needed some space or alone time, I would give it to him, but I'm so worried about him."

"You did the right thing, sweetie," Zoe said. "Men sometimes process death and grief differently than we do. They don't always want to talk about their feelings."

"I guess," Stella said. "But he loved Henry so much. The guy was like a father to him. He's hurting so much right now, and I don't know how to help him."

"Be there for him when he needs you," Jocelyn said before leaning over and kissing Stella's forehead. "Give him space when he asks for it. Ford loves you, honey. You'll get through this, I promise."

* * *

STELLA CLOSED THE FRONT DOOR OF HER TOWNHOUSE AND leaned against the door. She rubbed at the skin under her eyes before taking off her jacket and hanging it on the hook. Being with her family had been just what she needed but her stomach was still in knots. Her worry for Ford was making her almost physically ill. She slipped out of her boots and trudged up the stairs toward her bedroom. After leaving her parents, she wanted to stop at Ford's place but forced herself to drive home.

He didn't want company right now, and she wouldn't take that personally. It had been almost four days since Henry died, and they hadn't spent a single night together. She saw him at work, and they ate lunch together like they always did, but he declined every one of her offers to come to his place after work.

Don't take it personally, Stella. It has nothing to do with you.

She flicked the light on in her bedroom. Her brain knew that, but her heart was an emotional wreck. Tomorrow would be one of the worst days of Ford's life, and she desperately wanted to be with him tonight. She wanted to –

"Hey, Stella."

She screamed and staggered back, tripping over the laundry hamper and landing on her ass with a heavy thud. Ford jumped up from his spot on her bed and hurried over. "Honey, I'm sorry. I didn't mean to scare you."

He picked her up off the floor, and she stared wide-eyed at him as he rubbed her back. "Honey, are you hurt?"

She shook her head. "N-no, I just – you scared me."

"I'm sorry."

"Why are you sitting in my bedroom in the dark?" she asked.

"I miss you," he said.

"I miss you too," she whispered.

He hesitated before leaning down and kissing her. She returned his kiss eagerly, wrapping her arms around his waist and clinging to him. His soft kiss became deeper, his tongue sweeping past her lips to taste her. He reached for her shirt, and she touched his chest tentatively.

"Are you sure this is what you want?" she said.

It had been over five days since they'd been together, and her need for him was already at a boiling point. But she didn't want to force him into something he didn't want.

"Yes," he said. "Please, Stella. I need you so much."

He pulled her shirt over her head and cupped her breast through her bra, kneading it gently as they kissed again. They undressed each other, and Ford led her to the bed, urging her to lie on her back. He knelt on the floor next to the bed and wrapped his large hands around her thighs.

"Ford," she said breathlessly, "you don't have to do this. Let me make it about you tonight."

He shook his head before placing her legs over his broad shoulders. "No. This is what I want. What I need."

He bent his head and buried his face in her pussy before she could argue. She moaned and clutched at his head as he licked her clit into a swollen, throbbing bundle of nerves. Her heels drummed helplessly against his naked back as he licked and sucked and drove her relentlessly toward her climax. Shamefully, it didn't take long. She cried his name, her body arching off the bed as she came.

When she collapsed on the bed, he wedged his large body between her smooth thighs. He pushed inside of her and groaned. He propped himself up on his forearms, and she cupped his face and kissed him. She could taste herself on his lips, and she licked his mouth before smoothing her hands along his wide shoulders.

He pumped slowly back and forth, moaning quietly with every stroke. When he turned his face away, she cupped his jaw again and turned it back toward her.

"Look at me, honey," she whispered.

He stared steadily at her as their bodies moved together slowly and gently. His hard chest rubbed against her nipples, and she moaned in pleasure. Without breaking his gaze, he moved harder and faster. Ford was beginning to pant, and she watched in fascination as he bit his bottom lip and groaned.

"Stella," he whispered.

"Ford," she said before lifting her head and kissing him gently. He cried out into her mouth as his hips thrust furiously. She kept one hand on his face and clung to his shoulder with the other as he grew closer to his release.

BROKEN

"I love you, Stella," he rasped.

"I love you too," she said.

He shouted hoarsely, his entire body arching against hers as he drove her into the mattress a final time. She kissed the thick cords standing out in his neck as he shouted again, and warmth flooded through her. He kissed her face and mouth repeatedly before rolling off of her and collapsing on the bed next to her.

She curled into him, throwing her leg over one muscled thigh and putting her arm around his waist.

"I'm sorry," he said.

"You have nothing to be sorry about," she said.

"I shouldn't have pushed you away like I did."

"You didn't." She kissed his chest and smiled at him. "You needed some space. I understand that."

He sighed. "I wanted to be with you, but I didn't want to bring you down, I guess."

"Ford," she sat up and stared at him, "I love you and want to be with you no matter your mood. Okay? You miss Henry and are sad, but that's perfectly natural. I don't want you to pretend to be happy or think you need to stay away from me when you're not. I love you, and that won't change depending on your mood."

He smiled at her, and she leaned over him and kissed him. "I love you, Ford Taylor."

"I love you, Stella Johnson."

"I know. I'm irresistible."

He smiled again, and she rubbed her nose against his. "Will you stay the night with me?"

"Yes."

"Good," she said. They climbed under the covers, and he rested his head on her chest. "Do you want to talk about Henry, honey?"

She waited for him to tell her no, but Ford nodded. "Yeah.

I don't want to talk about him being dead or the funeral. I want to tell you about all the things he did for me when I was growing up. Okay?"

"Yes," she said before kissing the top of his head. "Tell me everything."

* * *

"Mom? Jocelyn? What are you doing here?" Stella said.

"We wanted to support Ford," Zoe said. "Your brother couldn't leave work, and your father is home with Ethan and Julie. Otherwise, they would have come as well."

"Thank you for coming to the funeral," Stella said before hugging them both. "I know Ford will appreciate it."

"How's he holding up?" Jocelyn asked.

"It's been rough for him, but -"

"Zoe? Jocelyn?"

Zoe turned at the sound of Ford's voice and hugged him. "I'm so sorry for your loss, dearest."

Ford returned her hug gingerly. "Uh, thank you."

Zoe smiled up at him and cupped his face. "If you ever need to talk, I'm a very good listener. Just ask my girls."

"She is," Jocelyn said as she squeezed Ford's arm. "I'm sorry about Henry, Ford."

"Thanks, Jocelyn," Ford replied. Zoe let him go, and he moved to Stella's side and put his arm around her waist. "Thank you both for coming."

"You're welcome, dearest," Zoe said. "Jocelyn and I are going to sit down. We'll talk to you after the service."

"Thanks, Mom," Stella said.

Her mother and sister walked away, and Ford said, "It was nice of them to come to support you."

"Not me, honey. You," Stella said. "They came for you."

He studied her for a moment. "Why would they do that?"

"Because you're part of our family, Ford."

His arm tightened around her waist, and she rubbed his broad chest. "You're not alone anymore, honey. You'll never be alone again. Okay?"

"Stella, I -"

"Hello, Ford."

Stella watched in confusion as all the blood drained from Ford's face. The look he gave her was near panic before he slowly turned around. Suzanne and another woman were standing behind them. The woman was slender, had dark hair and eyes, and was extremely pretty. She looked Stella up and down, her gaze lingering on Ford's hand around her waist.

"What are you doing here?" Ford said in a low voice.

Suzanne scowled at him. "Diana is my best friend, Ford. She practically grew up in our house, and she loved Henry."

Ford stared blankly at the woman. After a moment of awkwardness, Stella held out her hand. "Hi, I'm Stella Johnson, Ford's girlfriend."

Diana looked her up and down again before briefly shaking her hand. "It's nice to meet you."

"It's nice to meet you too," Stella said.

Ford was still staring at Diana, the look of panic growing on his face.

"It's good to see you again, Ford," Diana said. "It's been a long time."

"We have to go." Ford took Stella's hand in a hard grip and nearly dragged her away from Diana and Suzanne.

"Ford? Honey, what's wrong?" Stella said.

He shook his head. "Nothing. I just... nothing, Stella."

* * *

"Is it just me, or does that woman keep staring at Stella?" Jocelyn asked in a low voice.

"I thought it was just me," Zoe said. "Who is that woman, dearest?"

"Her name is Diana," Stella said. "She's Suzanne's best friend."

"Why does she keep staring at you?"

"I have no idea," Stella said. "I met her before the service, and Ford acted extremely weirdly around her."

"Weird, how?" Jocelyn asked.

"Like he was going to throw up, weird," Stella said.

Jocelyn studied the dark-haired woman thoughtfully. "Maybe they dated? Did Ford ever mention her?"

"No, but he's never mentioned any previous girlfriends," Stella said.

She sighed and set down her plate of uneaten food. After the service, the mourners had gathered at Ford's parents' house for refreshments. She glanced at her watch. It had been a few hours, and almost everyone had left.

"Ford's family has a lovely home," Zoe said. "Although," she lowered her voice, "it's a bit sterile feeling. I introduced myself to his parents earlier. I know they're grieving, so I won't judge, but they weren't very receptive when they found out who I was."

"Sorry, Mom," Stella said. "They kind of hate me, which probably extends to my family as well."

"Well, to be fair, I probably wouldn't like someone who threatened to punch my child in the face either," Zoe said.

"She deserved it," Stella said.

"Oh, undoubtedly." Zoe kissed Stella on the cheek. "Are you okay if we leave, dearest? I'm sure Julie will be hungry by now and your father is wonderful, but he never did get the hang of bottle feeding."

"Yes. Thanks for coming." Stella hugged her mother and then her sister.

"You're welcome, dearest. Will you give our love to Ford?" Zoe said.

Stella nodded and waved goodbye as her family left the room. She threw her plate of half-eaten food in the garbage before searching the room for Ford. He was nowhere to be seen. Only Ford's family, Diana, and a couple of people she hadn't met were in the room. She was about to leave to find Ford when Diana crossed the room toward her.

"Hello," Stella said.

"Hi there. I'm sorry, I've forgotten your name," Diana said.

"Stella."

"Right, Stella. You're dating Ford?"

"Yes," Stella said.

"How long have you been dating?"

"A few months."

"How did you meet him?"

"We work in the same building."

Diana stared silently at her, and Stella cleared her throat. "If you'll excuse me, I -"

"Stella!" Ford appeared out of nowhere, putting his arm around her waist. "What, uh, what are you doing?"

"We're just talking," Diana said. "Is that a problem, Ford?"

"No. Why would it be a problem?" Ford said. His hand dug painfully into her ribs, and Stella flinched.

"Honey, ease up."

"I'm sorry," he said. "Did I hurt you?"

"It's okay," she said.

"My brother never did know his own strength." Suzanne joined them. She was weaving slightly, downing the amber liquid in her glass before tossing the empty glass carelessly onto the couch.

"You're drunk, Suzanne," Ford said. "Go upstairs and sleep it off."

She ignored him and stared bitterly at Stella. "Threaten to punch anyone in the face lately?"

Stella bit her tongue as Suzanne laughed and threw her arm around Diana's shoulders. "She got mad because I wanted to know how much Ford paid her to pretend to be his girlfriend. You know something about that, don't you, Diana?"

"Be quiet, Suzanne," Diana said with a nervous look at Stella.

Ford's hand was pressing painfully into her ribs again, and Stella frowned. "Honey? What's wrong?"

"Nothing," he gritted out. "We need to leave."

"Not so fast," Suzanne said. "Are you telling me this pretend girlfriend doesn't know about your first pretend girlfriend?" She paused before laughing. "I guess girlfriend isn't the most accurate term."

"Suzanne!" Diana said. "Enough!"

"What? If she is his girlfriend, she won't care about his dirty little past."

Ford was staring at Diana. "You told her?"

"Of course, she told me, you idiot," Suzanne said. "I was her best friend. You really think she would keep something like that from me?"

"Ford? What is she talking about?" Stella said.

"Holy fuck, you really don't know, do you?" Suzanne said.

"Know what?" Stella said.

"Please, Stella," Ford said frantically. "Let's just go and -"

"When my brother was younger, he paid Diana to have sex with him," Suzanne said. "Shit, he pretty much paid for her entire university degree. Didn't he, Diana?"

Stella stared up at Ford. His face had gone from deathly

pale to bright red, and he gave her a heartbreaking look of shame as he dropped his arm from her waist.

"It took him a while to convince her," Suzanne said. "Hell, he practically begged her to fuck him. Isn't that what you said, Diana?"

Diana didn't reply, and Ford stepped back as Suzanne said, "It wasn't until he offered to pay her that she finally agreed to it."

She smiled cruelly at Ford. "Diana told me all about it, Ford. How she made you look away when you were fucking. How you started to think that maybe you could have an actual relationship with her. How you fell in love with her."

She laughed again. "Did you really think someone like her would fall in love with someone like you? Did you honestly believe that a woman who was being paid to fuck your ugly face would ever want to truly be with you?"

"Shut up," Stella said in a low voice as Ford backed away. "Ford, honey, don't -"

"How many other women did you pay to have sex with you after Diana ended it?" Suzanne asked.

Ford didn't reply, and Suzanne made another ugly laugh. "You're pathetic, big brother. Ugly and pathetic."

Ford gave Stella another look of shame. "I'm sorry," he said. "I'm so sorry."

"Ford -"

He turned and ran out of the room. Her stomach twisting, Stella stared at Suzanne.

"So," Suzanne said with a soft smile, "how much did my brother pay you to fuck him? I'm sure the price has gone up with inflation. Did you -"

Without saying a word, Stella balled her hand into a fist and punched Suzanne in the face. Suzanne staggered back and fell on her ass as blood gushed from her nose. Dylan and her parents rushed across the room toward them as Diana stared wide-eyed at Stella.

"Stay away from me and stay away from your brother, you miserable asshole," Stella said. She walked away without looking back.

* * *

"He's okay, Stella. He just needs time."

"It's been three days." Stella wiped at her swollen eyes as Jocelyn handed her more tissue. "He's not answering his cell phone, he hasn't gone to work, and he's not at home. I slept at his place last night because I thought maybe he was at least going home at night, but he never came home."

She burst into tears, and Jocelyn hugged her. "Sit down at the table, honey."

Stella sat at her small kitchen table and stared miserably at Jocelyn. "He's ghosting me, Jocelyn."

"He's embarrassed and upset. He's not ghosting you, honey."

"He is!" Stella insisted as Jocelyn pushed the steaming cup of tea before her. "He won't respond to any of my texts. I've lost track of how often I've texted or left him voicemails. I told him I didn't care about his past or what he did with Diana, but he still won't talk to me. I don't know what to do."

She started to cry again and then flinched when Jocelyn patted her swollen hand.

"Sorry," Jocelyn said with a grimace. "I forgot about your hand."

She grabbed a bag of frozen peas from the freezer before placing it in Stella's hand. "You really should go see the doctor about this."

"It's fine," Stella mumbled. "It's less swollen than it was."

"So, you punched Ford's sister in the face, huh?" Jocelyn said with a small grin.

Stella nodded, and Jocelyn's grin widened. "God, I wish I could have seen that."

"She deserved it. The things she said to him, Jocelyn. The look on Ford's face was so awful. He was so ashamed and – and – and..."

She burst into tears for the third time and wiped at her streaming eyes as Jocelyn rubbed her back.

"I just want to find him and tell him I love him," Stella said. "That I don't care about anything but being with him. But I can't do that if I don't know where he is. He could be alone and hurt somewhere."

"I'm sure he's fine. Maybe he's at a hotel," Jocelyn said.

"I swear I called every hotel in the city," Stella said. "None of them have a Ford Taylor registered as a guest."

Jocelyn sighed and patted Stella's shoulder. "He'll come back, honey. He has a job and a house. He can't stay away forever."

"What if he doesn't want anything to do with me when he returns?" Stella said. "What if he still won't talk to me? What if he doesn't want to be with me anymore?"

"He does," Jocelyn said. "Ford loves you, Stella."

"If he loves me, then why is he doing this? Why won't he talk to me?"

"He's embarrassed," Jocelyn repeated. "Honey, I don't know Ford very well, but it's obvious that he's sensitive. Having the woman he loves find out something like this had to be devastating to him."

"You didn't tell Mom or Dad, did you?" Stella said.

"Of course, I didn't," Jocelyn said.

"Ford's embarrassed enough. I shouldn't have even told you, but I had to tell someone, Jocelyn. I'm so worried about him."

"Honey, you know I'll never say a word to anyone, including Ford. Don't worry about that, okay?"

Stella nodded, and Jocelyn squeezed her shoulder. "Have you eaten today?"

"No."

"Let me make you something to eat."

"I'm not hungry."

"Stella -"

"I'm not hungry, Jocelyn. Please don't, okay?"

"Okay."

The doorbell rang, and Stella stared wide-eyed at Jocelyn. "Maybe it's Ford."

She jumped up and rushed out of the kitchen. She yanked the door open and could practically feel the hope dying in her body when she saw who it was. "What are you doing here?"

"I wanted to speak with you," Diana said.

"How did you know where I live?" Stella said as Jocelyn joined them at the door.

"I Googled you," Diana said. "Please, could we talk just for a few minutes?"

"I have nothing to say to you," Stella said. She started to swing the door shut, and Diana caught it with her hand.

"Please, Stella. Just ten minutes."

Stella glanced at Jocelyn, who shrugged. Stella sighed and opened the door. "Ten minutes."

Jocelyn grabbed her jacket from the hook and kissed Stella's cheek. "I'm going to go. Unless you want me to stay?"

"No, that's fine. Thanks, Jocelyn."

"You're welcome, honey."

She slipped past Diana and shut the door behind her as Stella stared silently at the dark-haired woman. After a moment, she said, "Come into the kitchen."

Diana followed her to the kitchen and sat down. Stella

sipped at her tea. "I'd offer you something to drink, but you're awful, and I hate you."

A small smile flickered across Diana's face. "I can see why Ford likes you."

"Shut up. You don't know anything about Ford or me," Stella said.

"No, I suppose I don't," Diana said with a small sigh. "Are you and Ford, uh, okay?"

"That's none of your business," Stella said. "If you're here just to find out the status of my relationship with Ford, you can get the fuck out."

"Yes, well, I'm guessing things aren't going well based on how awful you look."

"You're going to fucking insult me in my own home?" Stella said in disbelief. "You need to leave."

"No, wait," Diana said as Stella started to stand. "I'm sorry, that's not what I'm here for."

"What are you here for?"

"To apologize and to try to explain."

"I'm not interested. You owe Ford an apology, not me," Stella said.

"He's not returning my calls." Diana stared at the table. "I grew up poor. Suzanne and I met in high school and became best friends almost immediately. I was always a little envious of her wealth, I guess. After we graduated high school, I took out some student loans to go to university. It covered my tuition and books but not much else. I had a part-time job, but it didn't pay much."

Stella stared at her. Part of her wanted to tell Diana to shut the fuck up, but a bigger, stronger part of her was strangely fascinated.

"One night, I was at Suzanne's. We were drinking, and it didn't take long for her to pass out. I was tipsy but not drunk. I went downstairs, and Ford was in the kitchen. He had been somewhere overseas with the military for a few years, and he looked different. He'd always been a big guy, but being in the military had really," she paused, "toned his body. He was wearing jeans, and that was it. I'm not proud of this, but I remember thinking that if it weren't for his face, he'd be extremely fuckable."

Stella made a small sound of disgust, and Diana nodded. "Like I said, not proud of it. Anyway, I don't even know why Ford was there. His entire family hated him, and I was surprised he hadn't just rented an apartment or something. Maybe because he knew he wouldn't be there long before he went back overseas, so there wasn't much point in renting. Maybe he was hoping that his family would have missed him after being gone for a while."

She traced her fingertips across the top of the table. "I knew he'd always had a crush on me. He had never said anything, but I could see the way he looked at me when he thought I wasn't looking. It gave me an ego boost, you know? I don't know why. I'd already slept with my fair share of men, and I knew I was pretty."

Stella snorted, and Diana gave her an embarrassed look. "Maybe it was the alcohol, or maybe it was just my stupid ego, but I flirted with him that night. The look on his face – I can still remember it. It took him a while to figure out what I was doing. I don't think any girl had ever flirted with him before. Once he realized what I was doing…"

"What?" Stella said in a low voice.

"He was confused and – and wary almost, but there was this look of hope on his face, you know? Like he couldn't believe that I was flirting with him. It fed my ego even more, so I ramped it up. I started touching him, just light touches that could have been accidental. I think he nearly ran out on me a few times. He had no idea how to respond or what to do, and I thought it was kind of adorable."

"You're a monster," Stella said.

"Yes," Diana said. "I suppose back then I was. At the very least, I was cruel to someone who didn't deserve my cruelty."

She cleared her throat. "I had been flirting with him for nearly an hour when I got the idea."

"What idea?"

"What Suzanne told you isn't entirely accurate. I lied to her about it because I was ashamed," Diana said. "Ford didn't beg me to sleep with him, and he didn't offer me money. It was all my idea."

Stella stared wide-eyed at her. "Your idea."

"Yes. I knew Ford wanted to have sex with me. I knew he was probably a virgin, and I took advantage of him. It's not an excuse, but I really did need the money," Diana said. "Ford said no at first. It took me a couple of weeks to convince him. By then, he had gotten his own place. He was leaving in a few months, but he couldn't stand his family's coldness to him anymore. Suzanne and the rest of his family thought he was stupid and violent, but he wasn't. He was sweet, smart, and kind. I used that against him. I would show up at his apartment and tell him how broke I was and that I might have to drop out of school. I used his sweetness and his crush on me to get what I wanted."

Stella's stomach was churning, and for one brief moment, she thought she might throw up. She wanted to scream at Diana to shut up and get the fuck out of her house, but the words were stuck in her throat.

"Once he finally agreed, I told him I would teach him how to please a woman in bed," Diana said. "He was a fast learner and remarkably gentle. He was always so worried about his size and accidentally hurting me that teaching him to be gentle was easy."

Her face flushed, and she rubbed her forehead with a trembling hand. "I was cruel to him, though. I taught him to kiss, but once he was good at it, I refused to let him kiss me again. I would leave as soon as we were finished having sex. He initially asked me to stay a few times, but when I refused, he stopped asking. I made him look away when we were having sex. I told myself it was because he was ugly, but really, it was my own shame. I couldn't stand to look at him, knowing that he was falling in love with me despite my cruelty."

A strange smile crossed her face. "He was definitely all about giving me pleasure. I didn't have to teach him that. He was so eager to make me orgasm. He would spend hours just touching me and making me climax repeatedly."

Stella made a low choking noise. Diana glanced briefly at her before looking away. "He loved going down on me, but I refused to reciprocate. It was the one thing I wouldn't do and the only time he ever begged. He even offered me an extra thousand for just one blowjob, and I said no. I needed the money but wouldn't do it because I guess I... wanted to punish him somehow. I was the one who convinced him to give me money for fucking him, but deep down, I was so ashamed of my behaviour. Not going down on him and making him beg me for something I knew he desperately wanted was a way to make him feel as much shame as I did."

Stella was crying now, and Diana stared at her in embarrassment. "You want to know the ironic part? Ford was the best lover I've ever had. I'm ashamed of what I did to him, but I've spent the last ten years searching for someone who could make me feel as good as he did in bed."

"Get out," Stella said in a low voice.

"Stella, I know I have no right to ask this, but will you tell Ford I'm sorry? I was stupid and arrogant, and regret what I did to him. I really do."

"Get out," Stella repeated. "Get out of my house, and never contact me or Ford again."

"Will you tell him I'm sorry?"

"Get the fuck out of my house!" Stella shouted.

Diana flinched and stood up. "I – I'm sorry, Stella. Truly, I am."

She left the kitchen, and Stella burst into tears when the front door slammed shut.

* * *

"DO YOU HAVE PLANS FOR THE WEEKEND?" JASMINE ASKED.

"Camping out at Ford's house and hoping he comes home," Stella said.

"Stella, I'm worried about you," Jasmine said.

"I'm fine," Stella said. Jasmine was sitting with her in the atrium, and she tried to smile at her. "I'm just tired and really worried about Ford."

"Will you tell me what happened between you and Ford?" Jasmine asked.

"I don't want to talk about it."

Jimmy dropped into the empty chair at the table. "Good afternoon, ladies."

"Hi, honey." Jasmine gave him a quick kiss before rubbing Stella's arm. "Stella, I'm sure Ford is fine."

"I wouldn't know," Stella said. "He won't talk to me. I don't even know where he is, and he could be dead for all I know."

Jimmy shook his head immediately. "Jesus, he's not dead, Stella. He's fine. He just needs some more time to…"

He trailed off and gave Stella a nervous look when she studied him intently. "Do you know where he is, Jimmy?"

"What? No," Jimmy said. "Why would I know where he is?"

"Because the two of you are friends," Stella said. "Tell me where he is, Jimmy."

"I don't know where he is," Jimmy said.

"You're lying," Stella replied. "For God's sake, tell me where Ford is."

"Listen," Jimmy said desperately, "Ford is fine, okay? He's not -"

"Jimmy!" Jasmine snapped. "If you know where Ford is, you tell Stella right now, or I swear to God, I will never have sex with you again."

"Jazzy -"

"Don't Jazzy me," Jasmine said. "Tell her, Jimmy."

Jimmy sighed. "Fuck, Ford is going to fucking kill me. He's at my parents' cabin."

"Give me the address," Stella said.

"I can't!" Jimmy said. "Ford specifically told me not to tell you. If you show up there, he'll know that I -"

"Give me the goddamn address," Stella said.

"He'll be back on Sunday night," Jimmy said. "It's Friday, so you only have a couple more days. I'm sure the minute he gets back, he'll be at your house."

"Give her the address, Jimmy, or I will," Jasmine said.

"Ford is so going to kill me," Jimmy said.

"Forget Ford," Jasmine said. "I'll kill you if you don't tell her."

* * *

STELLA PARKED HER CAR IN FRONT OF THE SMALL CABIN. Ford's truck was parked next to it, and she breathed a sigh of relief as she climbed out of the car. She left for the cabin right after work despite the terrible roads. It was dark and snowing, and it had taken her three hours to get here. Her small car nearly slid off the road more than once, and she was tense and anxious over the drive and seeing Ford.

She waded through the deep snow toward the front door.

It opened, and she almost started crying when Ford appeared.

"Stella? What are you doing here?"

"I came to see you."

"You need to leave," he said.

She shook her head. "I'm not leaving until we talk."

"There's nothing to talk about," he said. "Just leave."

Her temper flared, and she glared at him before scooping up some snow. She packed it into a snowball and threw it at him. It hit him in the chest, and he stared at her in astonishment.

"Goddammit, Ford! I just drove three hours in a fucking blizzard and nearly died multiple times. I'm tired and scared and freezing my ass off! I miss you so much I can barely think straight, and you're telling me to leave? Fuck you! I'm not leaving!"

She whipped another snowball at him, and he ducked before starting toward her. Pissed off, she chucked more snowballs at him as he stomped through the deep snow. One hit him in the face, and he made a low curse before picking her up and tossing her over her shoulder.

She kicked and squirmed and pounded on his back. "I'm not leaving, Ford Taylor! You'll have to drag me kicking and screaming off this stupid mountain!"

"Stella, stop," he said. "I'm taking you into the cabin."

She stopped struggling and rested limply against him as he carried her into the cabin. It was toasty warm, and when he set her on her feet, she kicked off her boots and rushed over to the large fire crackling in the fireplace. She held out her hands and stomped her feet, wincing at the pins and needles going through her frozen toes.

Ford was staring warily at her, and she scowled at him. "I think my toes are frostbitten."

He picked her up again and carried her to the small

couch. He knelt in front of her and stripped off her socks before holding her feet in his large hands. "How does that feel?"

"It hurts," she said grumpily. "For every toe I lose to frostbite, I'm cutting off one of yours."

"You don't have frostbite," he said.

"You better hope I don't," she said.

He sighed and stared at her feet as he rubbed them briskly. "Why are you here?"

"Why am I here? Because I refuse to let you ghost me, you jerk," Stella said.

"Ghost you? What the hell does that mean?"

"It's when your boyfriend stops talking to you and never gives you an explanation. They dump your ass without being brave enough to tell you they're dumping your ass," she said.

"We both know you don't want to be with me anymore," he said. "I figured this would be easier. I was trying to be nice."

"Trying to be nice?" She sat forward and yanked her feet out of his hands. "Leaving me alone and not telling me where you're going is not being nice, Ford! I was worried sick about you."

"I'm sorry. I didn't think you'd be worried."

"I love you! Of course, I would be worried about you."

"You can't possibly love me after this."

"Ford," Stella leaned forward and cupped his face, "when I was nineteen, I slept with this guy I thought was my friend. I knew he didn't want to date me, but I was attracted to him and out of all the guys I knew, he didn't mind that I was fat. That was good enough for me. I gave him my virginity. Later, I discovered that he made fun of me to our other friends. He called me his 'fat girl mistake' and said that he only did it because he felt sorry for me."

He stared at her, and she squeezed his face. "Despite

knowing that, I slept with him three more times when he called me for booty calls. Do you know why? Because I was lonely, and even though I knew it was just a combination of pity and horniness on his part, I was tired of being alone. I know what it's like to be lonely."

"You don't," he said. "You think you do, but you don't, Stella. You didn't pay this guy to sleep with you. You didn't give him money just so that you would know what it was like to be with someone. You're not as pathetic as I am, and don't try to -"

"Diana told me the truth."

His look was guarded. "What do you mean?"

"Diana came to see me. She told me that she had lied to Suzanne and that what had happened between the two of you was all her idea. She said she used your sweetness and your crush on her against you because she needed money."

He dropped his gaze before shaking free of her grip. "It doesn't matter. I'm still a pathetic loser."

"Even if it had been your idea to pay her for sex, I would still be here. I'm not judging you for anything. Do you understand? You're not a pathetic loser," Stella said.

"I am!" he shouted. "You're the first woman to look at me without cringing. Once Diana was finished with me, I couldn't find a single woman to sleep with me. I still have no fucking idea why you're having sex with me! I want to be happy with you, I do, but every single fucking day, I wonder if this is the day that you finally wake up and realize you're too good for me."

"That's never going to happen."

"It will," he said. "Eventually, the stares and the whispers or the outright questions about why you're with me will wear on you, and you'll leave. You'll find someone who doesn't look like a monster, and you'll marry him and have a family with him."

ELIZABETH KELLY

"The only person I want to marry and have babies with is you. You're the most amazing man I've ever known, and I love everything about you."

"I can't be with you anymore. Don't you get that? Forget that you know how pathetic I am. I can't live every day wondering when you're going to leave. I just can't."

"I'm not going to leave," she said. "I love you, and I don't care about your past. I really and truly don't. If you call yourself pathetic or a monster again, I swear I'll punch you in the face."

He shook his head in disbelief, and she glared at him. "You don't believe me? Maybe you should call your sister and ask her how it feels to be punched in the face by me."

He blinked at her. "You punched Suzanne in the face?"

"Yes." Stella showed him her still-swollen knuckles. "Without you there to stop me, I went all Rocky Balboa on her ass."

He bent to kiss her knuckles before stopping abruptly and leaning away.

"Ford, listen to me carefully, okay? I don't care about your past. I love you," Stella said.

"Please just let me go, Stella," he said.

"No."

"Why are you doing this?"

"Because I love you and made a promise to Henry."

"What are you talking about?" Ford said.

"The day Henry came to see us, we talked about you and how much he loved you. He told me that you would try to push me away. He made me promise that I wouldn't let you. It's a promise I intend to keep."

His face twisted, and she cupped his face again before kissing him. "I love you. I will always love you, and I'm not letting you walk away from me, Ford Taylor."

"Stella," he whispered.

"I love you," she said again before pressing kisses all over his face. "I love you."

"I love you too," he said.

He yanked her into his arms, crushing her against his hard body as he kissed her. She returned his kisses frantically before reaching for the hem of his t-shirt. She pulled it over his head and ran her hands over his chest before pulling off her shirt and unhooking her bra.

"Stella, we should go to the bedroom," he moaned.

She shook her head and unbuttoned her jeans before pushing them and her panties down her legs. "Take off your pants."

He stripped them off, and she admired the way his cock stood out from his body before wrapping her hand around it. She stroked him firmly, and he moaned and slid his hand between her legs. He cupped her warm pussy, his fingers rubbing against her clit. She gasped and arched into his hand. He touched her lightly, and she clutched at his shoulders.

"Harder, Ford. Please."

"Whatever you want, honey," he said.

He stroked and tugged on her clit until she was crying his name and rocking against his hard palm. He watched as her orgasm swept through her, making her body shake and her cheeks flush.

She leaned against him and kissed his broad chest. "Lie on your back."

He laid on his back, and she straddled him, rubbing his cock with one hand as she traced his ab muscles with the other. "Just like the first time we made love. Remember?"

He nodded. "I'll never forget."

"Me neither," she said before rising up and guiding his cock to her wet entrance.

They both moaned as she sank down on him. His hands

cupped her hips, and she braced her hands on his chest. "I love you, Ford."

"I love you too, Stella."

She moved up and down with slow and measured strokes. He watched his cock disappear into her pussy and groaned. "Faster."

"Not yet, my love," she said.

She continued her slow and deliberate pace, watching as the look of lust on Ford's face deepened. When his hands bit painfully into her hips, she increased the pace, rolling her hips in a clockwise motion as she lowered her pussy down over his cock.

He groaned again and urged her to move faster. She took his hand and pressed it against her clit. "Touch me again."

He rubbed at her swollen clit, and she moved faster in response. He moaned and stroked her clit as she leaned over him and kissed him. He thrust his tongue into her mouth, and she sucked on it as she rode him hard and fast. His fingers were still rubbing her clit, and she screamed into his mouth as her second orgasm rolled through her. Her pussy tightened around his cock, and he moaned her name before pumping his hips furiously against hers.

She dug her nails into his chest and kissed him as he climaxed. His back arched, and she clung to him as he shuddered beneath her. She kissed his throat and his chest, and he wrapped his arms around her waist and buried his face in her neck.

"I love you, Ford," she breathed into his ear. "I love you, and I'll never stop loving you."

EPILOGUE

"Daddy?"

"Yeah, Sweetpea?"

"Am I smart?"

Ford smiled at the little girl as he tucked her into bed. "You're very smart."

"Am I funny?"

"Extremely funny," he said.

"Am I pretty?"

His gaze softened, and he stroked the little girl's red hair. "The prettiest girl I know, Sweetpea."

"Am I prettier than Mama?"

He hesitated, and the little girl grinned when she heard her mother's voice. "Answer carefully, honey."

Ford smiled at Stella as she walked into the bedroom. "Take your son, please."

She handed the baby to him, and Ford held him up in the air before nuzzling his belly. The baby giggled and grabbed his nose in a tight grip.

"Ouch! Not so tight, little man."

"He's strong like his dad," Stella said with a laugh before sitting on the edge of the bed.

"How was your day?" Ford asked.

"Good. I had an engagement photoshoot this morning, and a family shoot this afternoon," Stella said. "How was yours?"

"It was good. I was commissioned to do another portrait today. A family over on the west side." He tickled the little girl, and she giggled.

"Hi, Mama."

"Hi, Sweetpea. It's time to go to sleep."

"Daddy didn't answer me," she said.

Ford held the baby in the crook of his arm and stroked the little girl's hair again. "Well, considering you're the spitting image of your mama, I'd say it's a tie."

She smiled happily. "Daddy's handsome, isn't he, Mama?"

"Yes, Sweetpea, he is," Stella said. She kissed Ford on the cheek, and he put his arm around her waist. "But complimenting your daddy isn't going to extend your bedtime."

She pouted at them, and Ford laughed before tracing the freckles on her cheeks. "Go to sleep, Sweetpea. I love you."

"I love you too, Daddy. Night, Mama. I love you."

"I love you, baby girl," Stella said. She kissed the little girl and tucked the covers around her before taking Ford's hand and leading him from the bedroom. She shut the door, and they smiled at each other in the hallway. The baby yawned and dropped his head onto Ford's shoulder.

"Your turn to put him to bed," Stella said. "He needs a diaper change first."

Ford made a face, and she laughed before kissing him. "I'll be waiting for you in our bedroom."

He wiggled his eyebrows at her suggestively. "Will you be naked?"

She laughed again. "I might be."

Ford kissed the baby on his soft cheek and hurried down the hall. "C'mon, little man, it's time to get you to bed."

As he entered the nursery, she called his name, and he turned back to her.

"I love you, Ford."

"I love you too, Stella."

Keep reading for an excerpt from the novella "Always". Always tells the story of Stella's sister Jocelyn and is a low angst, sweet and steamy read.

Always will be available September 25, 2025.

ALWAYS EXCERPT

"Did Julie go to sleep okay?" Sawyer asked.

He was sitting at the kitchen table where she'd left him after they'd put Ethan to bed.

"She did." Jocelyn leaned against the counter. "Thank you again for being a part of Ethan's bedtime routine. It meant a lot to him that you read him his story."

"Happy to help," Sawyer said.

"Even though it means you'll have to take an Uber now rather than me driving you home?" she asked with a small smile.

"Even then," he said. "Thank you again for dinner. You're a great cook."

"I'm not sure you really got to eat much of it. Not with Ethan asking you questions every ten seconds and Julie stealing cheese off your plate every time you looked away."

Sawyer laughed. "I ate plenty."

"Well, I appreciate your patience with my kids."

"I had fun," he said. "They really are great. Also, Julie knowing sign language is very cool."

Julie had shown off a few of her signs over dinner, including 'eat', 'more', 'milk', and 'all done'.

"A lot of parents teach babies some basic signs," Jocelyn said. "It helps them communicate and can cut down on frustration while they're learning to talk."

Sawyer drank the last of his water before standing and joining her at the counter. He set the glass in the sink, and she studied the flex of his forearm and his hand with its surprisingly long fingers.

He smelled good. So damn good, and Jocelyn let her gaze drift across his upper body. The t-shirt he wore was tight, and she wondered what he would do if she traced her fingers across the hint of muscle she could see through the fabric stretched across his abdomen.

She raised her gaze to his, her body starting to ache with a need that had gone unfulfilled for too long. Sawyer studied her, his eyes darkening and his nostrils flaring. Desire - a desire for *her* - was evident on his face, and her body trembling, she quickly turned and opened a cupboard.

"Wine," she said, her voice too loud. "Let's have some wine."

Sawyer's hand covered hers before she could bring down the wine glasses from the cupboard. "Look at me, Jocelyn."

She swallowed hard and made herself turn. Sawyer reached for her before hesitating and letting his hand drop to his side. "It's getting late."

"It's only eight," she said.

"I can't stay any longer, and I can't drink wine with you, Butterfly."

"Why not?" she asked.

"Because it'll make me want to do things to you that friends don't do to other friends."

"What kind of things?" she whispered.

He leaned down until his mouth hovered just above hers. "Kissing."

One long finger traced her jawline and down her throat. "Touching."

"Sawyer," she breathed, her back arching when he traced her nipple through her shirt and bra.

"Finding out what colour your pretty nipples are," he said before leaning back and staring at her, his pupils blown wide. "Listening to you say my name as you come on my cock."

"Oh God," she said. "Those, um, those sound like very friendly things to do."

He grinned, and she would have been embarrassed by the ridiculousness of her comment if his need for her wasn't still so apparent. "Don't they?"

She took a deep breath. "I want those things too."